THE ABSENTEE KING

*The Medieval Saga Series
Book Five*

David Field

SAPERE BOOKS

Also in the Medieval Saga Series

Conquest

Traitor's Arrow

An Uncivil War

The Lion of Anjou

The Road to Runnymede

The Conscience of a King

THE ABSENTEE KING

Published by Sapere Books.

24 Trafalgar Road, Ilkley, LS29 8HH,
United Kingdom

saperebooks.com

Copyright © David Field, 2022
David Field has asserted his right to be identified as the author of this work.
All rights reserved.

No part of this publication may be reproduced, stored in any retrieval system, or transmitted, in any form, or by any means, electronic, mechanical, photocopying, recording, or otherwise, without the prior written permission of the publishers.
This book is a work of fiction. Names, characters, businesses, organisations, places and events, other than those clearly in the public domain, are either the product of the author's imagination, or are used fictitiously.
Any resemblances to actual persons, living or dead, events or locales are purely coincidental.

ISBN: 978-1-80055-801-4

I

Robert Derby shaded his eyes against the glaring sun as he heard horses approaching the entrance to the manor yard, then cursed quietly with the realisation that the lord and lady who owned the Repton estate were arriving. He had enough to do supervising the loading of the timber onto the cart so that it could begin its lumbering journey to the sawmill at Swarkestone, further downriver, but his brother Thomas, who had taken over after the deaths of their parents, had been insistent that he be prepared to welcome their superiors — preferably looking as neat and tidy as befitted the son of the estate steward.

Robert brushed the woodchips from his simple smock and muttered, 'Bloody rich folk — nowt better ter do than waste the time've honest workers.' He then stood to attention as he'd been instructed, doffing his cap.

As the newcomers rode through the gate, and a stable boy scuttled out to take the bridles of their mounts, Steward Thomas Derby ran from the door of the manor house in his anxiety to welcome them home. They hadn't set foot in here together for a long time, but fourteen years previously the grey-haired man now riding through the front gate — the master, the Earl of Repton — had made a brief visit. He'd been accompanied not by the lady now riding alongside him, but by a nurse and a baby boy, both of whom had been left for his late father Matthew to supervise. The master had only been back once in the subsequent years in order to enquire as to the boy's health and progress, and had been content in the knowledge that 'young Robert' had been absorbed into the family. Thomas had always feared that this day would come, but now that it had he was curiously calm — although his wife Meg would no doubt shed enough tears to rival the River Trent that glided along the southern boundary of the estate.

'Is that him?' the noblewoman asked of her companion as the two of them dismounted.

By this time, Thomas had reached them. 'That's 'im, beggin' yer pardon, milady,' he confirmed as he doffed his cap and executed a bow. 'There's bread, cheese and 'ome-brewed cider waitin' fer yer inside. Yer must be 'ungry after yer long ride from Lunnun. Then Meg — that's me wife — can set about showin' yer ter yer chamber, what's bin aired an' freshened this past week, ever since we got yer message.'

'We haven't exactly ridden all the way from London in one day,' Earl William said with amusement. 'We spent last night as the guests of the de la Zouche family in Ashby. They claim to be our nearest neighbours, although they pay homage to the Earl of Leicester, whereas my wife here is from the rival House of Chester. Perhaps surprisingly they didn't take the opportunity to poison us, so here we are. But that sturdy youth by the timber cart can't be Robert, surely? He can only be about fifteen years old, by my calculation.'

'Yer right, if 'e were less than a year old when yer left 'im 'ere that fust time,' Thomas confirmed. 'That were fourteen year ago now, an' we've told 'im that 'is birthday's the tenth o' May. So yeah, 'e's fifteen now, goin' on sixteen next May. But 'e's spent all 'is time workin' on the land, an' 'e's even stronger than me eldest, Peter, what's nineteen. We looked after 'im proper, just like I promised.'

'You did indeed,' Earl William confirmed, 'for which I thank you most profusely. As you can see, his mother can't take her eyes off him.'

All the time they'd been talking, Countess Adele had been staring, transfixed, at the burly youth who stood waiting by the cart to doff his cap when instructed. There was a catch in her voice as she quietly observed, 'He must be taller than his brother Hugh, and *he's* thirty years old, and a knight about to embark on a Crusade. Does Robert know of his true origins?'

'I'm afraid I never got around ter that,' Thomas replied sheepishly. 'By the time 'e were of an age when 'e'd understand, we wasn't sure if yer'd ever be comin' back again, so it were just easier ter let 'im think 'e were one've us. And in all ways what matter, 'e 'as bin. Meg's already breakin' 'er 'eart at the prospect've losin' 'im. It's like 'e's 'er favourite out've all the ones we've raised — five in all, countin' young Robert. And I'll fair miss 'im on the land, an' all — 'e's a good, strong lad, an' willin' wiv it. Always ready ter do what 'e's instructed, which can't be said fer everyone workin' on this estate.'

'How will he be likely to react to the news that we have to impart?' Adele asked, still unable to take her eyes off the youth, who was beginning to look uncomfortable under her fixed stare.

Thomas made a hesitant noise as he sucked air between his teeth. 'I couldn't honestly tell yer, an' that's a fact. The lad's never known any other life but the one on the estate 'ere, an' 'e's bin too much under the influence o' some've the village lads what's got no respect fer rich folk, beggin' yer pardon an' all. D'yer want me ter call the lad over?'

'No!' William replied quickly, then nodded towards his wife. 'I fear that his mother will be tempted to smother him with kisses, and the poor lad looks uncomfortable enough already. Best leave the introductions until tomorrow, when we've rested and Robert has been given the day off.'

Robert was duly advised that he was free to accompany the cart to the sawmill. Shaking his head as the visitors entered the manor house, he climbed onto the cart, which lumbered into motion when Ben Whittaker smacked the ox's rear with his long switch. 'Bloody daft rich folks, that thinks we're some sort've entertainment fer them,' Robert muttered. 'Still, mebbe there's a shillin' or more in it fer me if I carries on playin' the daft laddie.'

Once they had been left alone in the main — indeed the only — bedchamber on the upper floor of the manor house, Adele finally gave in to her tears. William held her close to his chest, suppressing a tear of his own as she choked out her words.

'It was as if he was a total stranger! The boy I gave birth to all those years ago in Poitiers — now he's grown into such a strong young man who I'd feel awkward holding in my arms…'

'Not half as awkward as *he'd* feel if you did,' William joked, hoping to ease her misery.

Adele wiped her face with the back of her hand, then grimaced. William fetched the cloth from the wash basin on the stand under the window, and she smiled her thanks. 'It must be just as bad for you — you're his father. Don't you feel like crying as well?'

'Of course I do, but I'm a man, and we don't,' he insisted.

Adele guffawed. 'I'm your wife, remember — I've seen you cry more than once.'

'That's as may be,' William replied, 'but it isn't going to help. To tell you the truth, I'm saving the tears for when he rejects us out of hand.'

'Why would he?' Adele asked, appalled. 'After all, we can offer him so much.'

'Perhaps not so much as the man he believes to be his brother,' William reminded her. 'He's settled here, part of a family, and knows only the ways of the land — how to manage a country estate. He has brothers and sisters whom he's grown up alongside, and a gentle couple who he thinks of as his brother and sister-in-law. How would you feel if someone had told you, at the age of fifteen, that you were a cuckoo who'd been brought up in a nest of swallows?'

Adele sat down heavily. 'Then what are we going to do? We're due in Marlborough next month, then we have to attend the coronation. And you have to take up your new duties in Westminster.'

'All we can do is tell him the truth,' William said. 'My concern is that the truth will not be to his liking, and that he'd prefer to stay exactly as he is. Perhaps the best we could offer, by way of a compromise, is that he can become the steward of the estate when Thomas passes on.'

'But he could have a life at court — a life of privilege, wealth, prestige, and so on.'

William frowned. 'Also duty, and fear of displeasing the king and falling out of favour. A life of intrigue, treachery and plotting, always waiting for a knife in his back.'

Adele's face fell. 'Is that how you see *our* life?'

William shrugged. 'Who knows? We have a new king, and we would seem to be in favour at present. But, as Eleanor's life has taught us, even being the queen does not guarantee you happiness, or even freedom.'

'Not every husband imprisons his wife the way Henry did Eleanor,' Adele argued. 'Richard at least respects his mother.'

'All I'm saying is that we may not be doing Robert any favours if we introduce him at court. Even assuming that he wants that, he'll have to wait until someone — presumably us

— teaches him the necessary manners and bearing. If he speaks anything like Thomas, he'll seem like a landed peasant.'

'We all still speak French at court,' Adele reminded him.

'And how much of that do you imagine Robert has been taught at the village school — assuming that he's had any schooling at all?'

Adele nodded sadly. 'So it seems that our youngest child is destined to remain here, while we trudge around after the dreary court, and Hugh risks his neck on Crusade, riding alongside that lunatic who thinks he's destined to save the world from Mohammedans. At least our daughter found a soft landing.'

'We won't know that until we see her again,' said William. 'It's been over a year since Joan and Ralph retired to their estate in Cornwall, and for all you know he's taken to beating her daily.'

'Don't!' Adele pleaded as tears began to shine in her eyes again. 'I've endured enough for one day, and I need to rest. We can only see what tomorrow brings.'

II

The next morning Robert was summoned into the parlour kitchen of the manor house, and told to take a seat opposite the lord and lady of the manor. He wasn't entirely surprised, since the atmosphere around the place had seemed odd ever since they'd ridden in, and his brother could barely look him in the eye. As for Meg, he'd been told by his sister Beth — a little accusingly, he thought — that she'd taken to her bed in the back room. Beth had heard her sobbing to herself when she'd brought in the milk from the parlour just before breakfast. Now Robert had been told that the owners of the estate wanted to speak with him, and he was apprehensive that his work hadn't been up to standard, and that he was to be banished from the estate.

As he sat with his eyes down on the table — showing what he'd been taught was 'due respect' to one's 'betters' — Lord William broke the silence.

'Robert, we have some very important things to tell you,' he began.

'I can work 'arder — honest! If yer just gives me a chance!' Robert pleaded.

Thomas placed a consoling hand on his shoulder. 'It's not that, lad — yer a grand worker. Just listen ter what the lord 'as ter tell yer, there's a good lad.'

Robert remained silent, and William continued.

'The first thing you have to know, Robert, is that Thomas here isn't your brother, and Matthew wasn't your father.'

Robert took that in, wondering if he was therefore one of those 'orphan' types who lived in the nearby priory and were only allowed off its premises once a week, to mingle with the children from the village school that he attended.

'You were brought here as an infant, less than a year old, by a nobleman who was living in a place called Poitiers, which is across the English Channel,' Lord William explained. 'Have you heard of Queen Eleanor, by any chance?'

Robert shook his head, wishing that he'd paid more attention at school instead of pulling Mary Porter's hair from behind.

'Well, this nobleman was adviser to Queen Eleanor, who'd escaped from the king, her husband.'

'Yer mean 'e were wantin' 'er dead?' Robert asked.

William shrugged. 'We needn't go into that just now. What I'm trying to tell you is that this nobleman was your father, and your mother was one of the queen's ladies.'

'Was they married?' Robert asked. 'Or am I one've them ... well, yer know? What me brother Peter calls Daisy the cow when she kicks 'im in the milking shed?'

'No, Robert,' William chuckled, 'rest assured that your parents were married, and still are. But they're back in England now, and they'd like you to rejoin their family, and meet your brother and sister. Your *real* brother and sister, that is.'

'Your older brother's name is Hugh. He's a knight, about to go on Crusade with the new King Richard,' Lady Adele told him. 'And you have an older sister called Joan, who's married to the Earl of Bodmin, and lives on her estate in Cornwall.'

Robert was clearly deep in thought, then surprised them all by enquiring of a glum-looking Thomas Derby, 'So if what them's sayin' is right, then Beth ain't me sister?'

'That's right,' Thomas confirmed as he forced a smile, deeply hurt that Robert hadn't responded to the devastating news with tears and protests. 'But do yer hate our family fer deceivin' yer all these years?'

'No,' Robert insisted, 'since yer've fed me, an' taught me 'ow ter run an estate, so I'm proper set up in life.'

An ominous silence was broken by a gentle response from William.

'Your real parents would like you to rejoin your *own* family, Robert, and learn how to behave in court, then perhaps become a nobleman yourself.'

Robert shook his head vigorously. 'Never!' he protested. 'Them rich folks doesn't know 'ow ter live a proper life — milk a cow, string a line've fences, bring in the 'arvest, an' suchlike. All they're fit fer's mincin' around an' livin' off the backs've the likes of me an' Thomas 'ere. Leastways, even if 'e's not me brother after all, an' I 'as ter call him summat else, 'e's the one what's taught me all I needs ter know in life, an' I'm stayin' 'ere.'

'No yer not,' Thomas insisted, although there was a catch in his voice. 'This 'ere gentleman's the lord've the manor, an' if 'e sez yer gotta go, then yer gotta go. If yer doesn't, then all've us — me, Meg — an' Peter, Benny, Sarah an' Beth — we'll all be 'omeless. The lord's word's law around 'ere, yer see.'

'But I've done nowt wrong!' Robert protested.

William nodded. 'Of course you haven't, but your real parents want you to join them at court.'

'Well, they can go an' fart in their fancy bonnets!' Robert announced angrily as he shot up from the table and headed for the door. 'I'll live rough in the woods, see if I don't! Then when I'm starvin' I'll sneak back, an' Beth'll feed me at the kitchen door!'

The parlour door slammed behind him, and Thomas looked, red-faced, across the table at William and Adele.

'I'm right sorry about that,' he mumbled sheepishly. 'We didn't bring 'im up ter talk like that ter gentry — or ter anybody else, fer that matter.'

William reached across the table to place a reassuring hand on his shoulder. 'I know you didn't, Thomas, and believe me when I say how grateful my wife and I are for everything you've done to raise such a strong and spirited youth. And what I have in mind will mean that he can remain here for the foreseeable future anyway.'

Thomas looked up with a hopeful expression, although he remained silent as William shared his thoughts.

'Robert's a strong, spirited lad, but he's clearly not ready for court yet. For one thing, there's his manner of speech. With all due respect to you and your family, it's not the way one speaks in the royal presence, or anywhere else in courtly circles. And what's more, they speak French. He needs to be educated to learn how we really live in noble society, which is not the way he's been led to believe by biased tongues in the village. All this means that he'll be here for a good few years more, if you'd be so kind as to continue to supervise his welfare in our absence.'

'O' course!' Thomas said, as a tear appeared in the corner of one eye. 'We've bin breakin' our 'earts ter think we'd be losin' 'im fer good, so what yer suggestin'd be like a blessin' from 'eaven. But weren't yer plannin' on bein' 'ere yerselves?'

'I'm afraid that our duties at court will be dragging us away again very shortly,' William admitted. 'You may not yet know, but we have a new king called Richard, and we'll be required at his coronation in our respective roles. The king's appointed me as Chief Justice of England, so I'll be required to tour the country trying offenders against the law. My wife here is still attendant on the Queen Dowager Eleanor, who's opted to remain here in England while Richard goes on Crusade, accompanied by our older son Hugh, who's one of his knights. But before the coronation, we're required at the marriage ceremony of the king's younger brother, Prince John, in Wiltshire. Is there any superior school in the locality? Other than the village school, I mean.'

Thomas nodded. 'There's a college of sorts at Repton Priory, where the sons've the gentry around these parts gets a schoolin' ahead of 'em going into the Church, or mebbe the law or summat. Would that do?'

'Probably. I'll ride over and speak with the prior, to tell him what we need Robert to be taught. I was raised in a similar priory school myself, so hopefully it will be adequate.'

'They charges money, or so I believe,' Thomas warned him.

William smiled. 'We're talking about our son, remember? Fortunately, the money won't be an obstacle.'

'But he doesn't yet know he's our son,' Adele reminded William.

He looked out through the narrow parlour window. 'Then it's about time he did,' he announced as he rose from the table.

William found Robert draped over a fence, staring at the oxen who were kept for ploughing and other farm work inside a narrow compound. The youth looked up with a resentful glare, and there were red marks down his cheeks where angry tears had only just dried. William stood next to him and chose his words carefully.

'You can stay here if you do as I say,' he told him. Robert didn't reply, so William pushed on. 'You're to go to school at the local priory, and learn things you'll need to know one day, when you take your rightful place at court.'

'And if I don't want any've that?' Robert asked defiantly.

William smiled. 'Then you can go and hide in the woods, as you threatened to do. But if you're prepared to do as I say, then you can stay here and continue to assist with the running of the estate. We need someone educated to take care of the books anyway.'

'And why should I do what yer says?' Robert asked.

'Because I'm the lord of this estate, and I say who stays here and who doesn't.'

'And what will my *real* parents 'ave to say about that? 'Ow does yer know they'll agree to it? Shouldn't they be 'ere, makin' all these decisions fer the rest've me life?'

'They're here already, Robert,' William told him as his eyes misted up. 'Whether you approve or not, I'm your father, and the lady making her way down here from the house is your mother. Prepare for the strongest hugs you ever experienced, and the loudest cries of joy you ever heard.'

III

'The Countess of Bodmin,' the page announced as he held open the doors to the rear ground floor chamber in Marlborough Castle, and in rushed an excited lady in her mid-twenties. She embraced her mother, Adele, Countess of Repton, with an enthusiasm strengthened by their recent separation. Adele wiped a tear from her eye as she stepped back to take a better look at her only daughter, then her eyes opened wide with surprise as she spotted the bulge in Joan's rich green gown.

'Yes — I'm with child!' Joan gushed. 'Your first grandchild!'

'The first *legitimate* one, anyway,' her father William added as he took his turn for a loving hug. 'Heaven alone knows what your brother Hugh gets up to in Richard's service.'

'Talking of brothers,' Joan asked, 'how went matters in Repton?'

'Middling well, we think,' Adele replied. 'Robert seemed to finally accept that we are his parents, and he has agreed to undertake schooling from the sub-prior of the local monastic house as a condition of his being allowed to remain and manage the estate. Unfortunately, he seems to have acquired rough ways that will render him unfit for presentation at court until he is the same age that you are now. But no matter — the important thing is that he is safe and well, and Repton will thrive under his supervision. But what of yourself? Does your husband share your pleasure at the impending birth? For that matter, when is it likely to be?'

'I'm five months gone, so the physician predicts a birth around Christmas time. Will you attend me?'

Adele's face fell slightly. 'That will depend upon where your father's duties take him. We have so much news to impart, following our arrival back in Portsmouth from Poitiers. You will recall that when King Henry died, leaving England and all the other possessions to Richard, he showed his gratitude for your father's assistance to his mother, the Lady Eleanor, by appointing him Chief Justice of England. He'd trust no-one else with the role, I believe. That is why we have been favoured with such grand chambers here in Marlborough Castle, while I suspect that you and Ralph are accommodated somewhere in a nearby abbey, or perhaps a more distant bishop's palace.'

'No,' Joan replied gleefully. 'You forget who my brother-in-law is. Ralph's brother Walter is of course the Archbishop of Rouen, as well as being the Bishop of Lincoln, and he has been of considerable service to Prince Richard in recent months. I don't pretend to know all the details, but seemingly he absolved him of all responsibility for the rebellion that led to King Henry's death, then invested him as Duke of Normandy. He then accompanied Queen Eleanor back across the Channel to Westminster, in order that she might take up her duties as the head of the Regency Council. But he will also be conducting the wedding ceremony of Prince John and Isabella of Gloucester, which is why we are all here. We've got a splendid set of first-floor chambers overlooking the fishponds, which Walter is sharing with us.'

'Surely the Archbishop of Canterbury should be conducting a ceremony as important as the marriage of a royal prince?' Adele queried.

William shook his head. 'The meeting I was called to this morning was with Chancellor Longchamp, who sought my legal opinion on the breach of precedent. So long as the marriage ceremony is conducted by an ordained priest, it does not matter in law whether he's the Primate of All England or some humble village mumbler. Archbishop Baldwin has dug in his heels against the marriage, on the grounds of consanguinity. It seems that Prince John and his intended bride are half-second cousins, or suchlike, since they have a common great-grandfather in the first King Henry.'

'How did that come about?' Adele asked.

'You will of course remember Robert of Gloucester, who was uncle to the late King Henry and adviser to his own half-sister Maude?' William went on. 'Well, seemingly Isabella is his granddaughter, and although her father was one of the first Henry's bastards, the bloodline is still there. Baldwin is taking a fine line of argument as part of his ongoing dispute with the Crown regarding his ambition to build a new church at Canterbury. Richard is livid with him, it seems, but as usual Walter de Coutances is proving his worth to the prince, and has agreed to conduct the ceremony.'

'I hear that Queen Eleanor has been singing his praises all over Westminster,' Joan added, 'since this royal marriage is important to her. Anyway, you must be aware of that, Mother, since the queen consults you about everything, and I hear that she has been in residence here for several days.'

'She is now only the *dowager* queen,' Adele reminded her, 'and I am her senior lady, not her adviser. But you are correct in your belief that I get to know a lot of what is on her mind, and it seems that she is not so enthusiastic about the proposed marriage of Prince Richard to Alys of France.'

'Because she is reputed to have lain with his father?' Joan asked eagerly.

Adele shook her head. 'It is, I believe, more the case that she has identified a better prospect for the hand of her favourite son. Anyway, talking of my mistress, I must make my way to the kitchens to ensure that her dinner contains nothing that would be likely to upset her delicate digestion, which has been betraying her of late. It's probably all that extensive travel, although she is now in her sixty-seventh year, which is in itself quite an achievement.'

'Not so great an achievement as yours,' Joan grinned, 'giving birth to my baby brother Robert when you were forty-two years old.'

Adele blushed. 'That *was* totally unexpected, of course, but I'm not the only one to have survived such an experience. Apparently it would have been much worse, had I not had you and Hugh before that. Or so my physician told me, and he was of course the finest in Poitiers. Anyway, I must leave you. No doubt your father will want to hear more about the triumphs of your illustrious brother-in-law.'

'Not really,' William admitted as the door closed behind her, and father and daughter sat beside each other in the window alcove overlooking the courtyard that led to the rear stables. 'However, I *would* like to learn more of the dispute between Prince Richard and Archbishop Baldwin.'

'I've told you all I know,' Joan shrugged, 'but *your* news is far more exciting! What will be your new duties?'

'I have no real idea, to be perfectly honest,' he admitted. 'The title is "Chief Justice of England". So far as I can make out, this places me at the head of all those who travel the nation in the king's name, enforcing the criminal law. I only have myself to blame for that, since I was the one who introduced the system when I advised King Henry all those years ago. But your mother was closer to the truth than she imagined when she said I am the only man that Richard could trust with the job. It seems that he is intent on departing the land as soon as he is crowned, and taking your brother Hugh with him to the

Holy Land on Crusade. He fears that in his absence his younger brother John will seek to increase his power in England by creating chaos and fermenting crime.'

'According to Walter, John has pledged to remain across the Channel until Richard's return,' said Joan.

'He also promised his father he wouldn't join the other brothers when they rebelled against him, but when he judged the moment to be right he journeyed to Paris, where he nestled under the wing of the poisonous King Philip.'

'But surely their mother will be ruling the country, and will prevent John doing anything behind Richard's back?'

William sighed heavily. 'Were I asked the question, I would be hard put to decide which of Eleanor's youngest sons is the true favourite — Richard or John. She clearly has strong ties to them both, having given birth to them. But I know nothing of motherly feelings, clearly, and fatherly ambitions are, I suspect, of a different order altogether.'

'Are you happy that I am shortly to bear your first grandchild?' Joan asked coyly.

'Of course, although it serves to remind me of my great age. I will be sixty-five on my next birthday, although there are times these days when it feels more like *eighty*-five. I hope I do not become one of those old dodderers who outlives his body.'

'You are fortunate that you owe your preferment to the cleverness of your brain,' Joan agreed, 'and do not have to risk your life on the field of battle. I fear for Hugh when he rides alongside Richard in the deserts of the East. But surely England will not be governed merely by Queen Eleanor? Ralph tells me that there is a council advising her.'

William's response was a hollow laugh. 'Indeed there is, and it consists of men who paid for their positions. Richard sold off the highest offices in England in order to raise the money for his precious Crusade. Then he raided the Treasury, so the nation will be in poverty as well as being without a king for as long as he dallies overseas. I will feel happier if you remain securely on your Cornwall estate for the foreseeable future, producing grandchildren. Please try to persuade Ralph not to engage in any intrigues — with *anyone*, however compelling their promises.'

'I would obviously prefer that, Father, so do not doubt my efforts to ensure that we enjoy a long and happy marriage. Talking of which, I am required upstairs for dinner — will you join us at board?'

William shook his head. 'I will dine here alone with my gloomy thoughts.'

IV

The wedding of John, Prince of England and Count of Mortain, and Isabella, Countess of Gloucester, took place inside the chapel of Marlborough Castle on 29th August 1189. They had been betrothed for almost thirteen years, and by this marriage the largely landless John would become the absolute Earl of Gloucester, due to his father's deliberate disinheritance of Isabella's two sisters. In addition, Richard had sought to buy his younger brother's allegiance by granting him wide estates in six English counties, although he had tactically retained military control of any strategically important castles in those regions.

If John was elated at this conclusion to a lengthy period of betrothal, it was not obvious in his mulish face as he took the marriage vows in a tone of resignation. Unusually for such marriages of dynastic convenience, there was no yawning age gap between the parties — the bride was only sixteen and John was not much older, at twenty-three years of age. Given his immaturity, they were an even match.

William, by virtue of his exalted office, was in the first row of the nave, barely a few feet from the couple as they stood taking their vows before God and under the smug gaze of Walter de Coutances, Bishop of Lincoln on this occasion. Even though John's back was to him, William was reminded of how much he took after his father, while Richard had been blessed with their mother's lofty elegance. Whereas Richard was well over six feet in height, but slimly built with a rich head of fair hair and matching beard, John was by comparison almost squat, with his father's powerful barrel chest and dark red hair. He was rumoured to have also inherited the paternal temper, as well as a love for the hunt in all its forms. Should he become king as the result of any accident befalling Richard during his planned warfare in the Holy Land, England could expect to be plunged back into those dark days of unpredictable rages that William remembered so well.

It was therefore with a sense of foreboding that William left Marlborough ahead of the main exodus back to Westminster, leaving Adele to accompany Eleanor at a more leisurely pace. He was anxious to establish himself in his new chambers alongside the Great Hall in which he intended to preside as the resident judge for all trials of national significance, such as plaints for treason or sedition. He had already interviewed several promising candidates for positions as senior clerks, and had appointed a Berkshire noble, Sir Gervais Montjoy, as his registrar. At present, his pending trial list reflected more local matters, such as murders and rapes that had occurred in the murky, twisted confines of the old city to the east, with its wharfs, warehouses, taverns, brothels and densely packed residences. But before he could give serious attention to any of these, he would be required to attend his first meeting of the Regency Council, even though Richard was still in London, and Queen Dowager Eleanor was devoting most of her time to the meticulous arrangements for the coronation and the subsequent banquet — which would take place in the same Great Hall of Westminster in which William would be condemning the guilty to hang at Smithfield.

He experienced a profound feeling of depression at the commencement of the first meeting of the Regency Council. He took his place down one side of the long table that had been dragged into the Council Chamber on the first floor, around which sat so many of those who had paid for the privilege of being there. It was of no comfort to him to note the reassuring presence of Queen Eleanor at the head of the table in her role as Regent, given that next to her sat the biggest opportunist of them all, William de Longchamp, who occupied the prestigious offices of Co-Regent, Chancellor and Joint Chief Justiciar, and was therefore the office bearer under the Crown to whom William would be answerable as Chief Justice.

There was no doubt that Longchamp's current favoured status owed much to the sycophantic forelock-tugging and obsequious bowing and scraping that previous generations of his family had bestowed on the line of English monarchs who had succeeded Duke William of Normandy, in whose train de Longchamp's great-grandfather had ridden from Normandy in his chainmail.

They had subsidised their sycophancy with astute marriages, and de Longchamp was now related to the de Lacy dynasty. He had entered the public service as an official in the office of Geoffrey, Archbishop of York, one of the several illegitimate sons of the former King Henry, before sniffing the wind for long enough to enter the Chancery of Aquitaine during the years in which Richard had been its duke.

He'd rapidly became one of Richard's trusted advisers, and had allegedly contributed three thousand pounds towards Richard's war chest in return for his appointment as Chancellor of England. In that role he had further ingratiated himself with Richard by emptying the Treasury of the proceeds of the Saladin Tithe — a tax imposed on the nobility by King Henry in the days when he had contemplated embarking on a Crusade himself. De Longchamp was the reason why England was now all but bankrupt, and his rewards were the three offices for which he had neither the experience nor the ability.

For good measure, he was also about to become the Bishop of Ely.

But he was by no means the only one whose head ought to have been hung in shame as they sat waiting for Queen Eleanor to announce what business needed to be conducted. The other justiciar was Hugh de Puiset, Bishop of Durham, who had become Earl of Northumbria for two thousand pounds, and Joint Justiciar of England for an additional thousand. If he was embarrassed to be holding conflicting offices in the manner of Becket before him, it didn't show in his self-satisfied grin, although his occasional hooded glares at de Longchamp across the table gave early warning that their tandem occupation of the Justiciar's role would not be an amicable one.

Also there by dint of financial contribution to the retaking of Jerusalem were Hugh Bardulf, a former steward to the royal household of the late King Henry, William Briwere, a Devon clergyman, Geoffrey FitzPeter, High Sheriff of Northamptonshire, and a young knight errant called William Marshall, who was about to become Earl of Pembroke through an advantageous marriage.

William was even less reassured by the total silence around the table. These were men who knew each other well — they had met on many prior occasions, and were now at the centre of power — but they exchanged none of the low, murmured asides that were normal at the start of meetings, before they were called to silence by whoever was presiding. Either they had nothing to say to each other, or they chose to keep their counsel. They did not even make eye contact, and each gaze was focused on the surface of the table as Queen Dowager Eleanor raised her head to speak.

'There are only two matters that I wish to announce this morning,' she told them with an expression that discouraged argument. 'The first is that my son Richard has requested that his brother John remain in England when he departs on Crusade. The second is that shortly before he does so, he will be naming his nephew Arthur as his heir.'

William looked quickly down the table for the immediate reactions of those around it. William de Longchamp's face resembled that of a man who had just been advised of the death of a close relative, while Hugh de Puiset smiled quietly into his beard, although it was impossible to guess which of the announcements had provoked these reactions. But in William's estimation, both proposed actions could prove disastrous for the nation.

Prince John had ever been jealous of all his brothers, but none more than his immediate older brother Richard, who had not only inherited all the good looks, charisma and martial skills, but had always been their mother's favourite. John had proved himself to be slimy and treacherous when first seeking to ingratiate himself with their father — in the hope that he would inherit everything by being the only loyal son — then joining the rebellion against him when his initial tactic failed to gain him the pre-eminence he craved. He was hardly likely to remain in England without seeking to undermine Richard's authority in his absence, perhaps by becoming their mother's new favourite. Indeed, it was possible that he'd done so already, and that it had been Eleanor who had persuaded Richard to make such a rash decision.

Then there was the potential for unrest created by the naming of Arthur as heir. Arthur of Brittany was the four-year-old son of Geoffrey, born after his father's death during a tournament in Paris. Geoffrey had been the third son born to

Henry and Eleanor, and the only one to leave a legitimate male heir. Arthur was ruling as Count of Brittany under the regency of his mother Constance, a formidable lady who was ambitious for her son, and equally so for his older sister Eleanor. It was difficult to imagine John meekly accepting that he had been publicly snubbed yet again by a close family member. Therefore, it was likely that he would plot to have little Arthur, and perhaps also his mother, taken out of the reckoning.

'If no-one wishes to make any observation on these matters,' Eleanor announced as she rose sedately to her feet, requiring all those present to rise also, in addition to bowing, 'then I have much to see to regarding the coronation arrangements.' With that, she turned and exited the chamber through the private door to the rear that led to the royal quarters, leaving a stunned silence behind her.

William was one of the last to leave the chamber. He was barely a few yards down the public corridor when he felt a restraining hand on his sleeve, and turned to find the grim face of William de Longchamp staring into his.

'What thought you of those pronouncements?' de Longchamp asked.

William shrugged. 'Time will tell, obviously, but neither of them bode well for the peace of the nation.'

'My thoughts entirely,' de Longchamp replied with a nod. 'But you will, in the discharge of your duties, be well placed to stamp out any lawlessness provoked by those seeking to undermine the rule of our soon to be King Richard, will you not?'

'I shall endeavour to suppress *all* crime, whomsoever it is provoked or performed by,' William assured him in what he hoped was a non-committal response to the political implications of the original question. De Longchamp's face darkened as he leaned in and lowered his voice.

'I do not trust John Lackland, William. He was ever resentful of the favours shown to his older brothers, and his soul is as black as a monk's cowl. I shall look to you to discover his hand behind any criminal conspiracies, or spates of riotous and unruly behaviours, designed to make him appear the more suitable to rule England. Do we understand each other?'

'Understand this, at least,' William replied as he wrestled with his rising temper, 'I have been appointed to deal with *all* crime. I shall do so without fear or favour, and without partiality or well-meaning advice such as yours. On the morrow, I am slated to preside over a case involving the violent rape of a twelve-year-old serving girl by the crew from an Italian wool vessel that lay moored at Shadwell. I shall have no regard for the fact that those accused are Italian, nor shall I allow myself to be bribed by their attorneys to guide the jury to an outcome favourable to those accused — who, if found guilty, I shall sentence to hang. In the event of any guilty finding, I do not propose to enquire who inspired or encouraged them to commit such a heinous act. Now, do *we* understand each other?'

'You have much to learn,' de Longchamp muttered as he turned to leave. 'You can only hope that it is to your advantage, and your continued office.'

Hardly anyone in the kingdom had ever laid eyes on the man who was about to become their new king. The crowds therefore pressed eagerly forward — many of the weaker ones were pushed aside, or forced to the ground — as the splendid procession wound its way into the ancient Abbey of Westminster, founded by the last Saxon king to make London his base. Bishops, abbots, barons, knights and nobles who had shamelessly paid for the privilege formed a long line that passed solemnly through the west door with Prince Richard at its centre. It progressed to the altar, those making up the original procession peeling off in the process in order to take their seats in the nave. This left only Richard and a handful of bishops to approach the altar, on which were laid the royal regalia, a gilt bible and various holy relics, and behind which stood Baldwin of Exeter, Archbishop of Canterbury.

Richard's voice rang clearly and confidently as he knelt before the altar and swore on the holy relics before him. 'I will all the days of my life observe peace, honour and reverence towards God, the Holy Church and its ordinances. I will exercise true justice and equity towards the people committed to my charge, and will abrogate bad laws and unjust customs, if any have been introduced into this, my kingdom, and will enact good laws, observing same without fraud or evil intent.'

Three rows back down the nave, William offered up his own silent prayer that these vows would be honoured as he watched Richard being stripped down to his shirt and hose, prior to the archbishop anointing his head, chest and arms with holy oil and pronouncing a Latin blessing. Then once Richard had been reclothed in consecrated linen and royal robes, he was handed his symbolic sword of office. Two earls who had no doubt paid handsomely for the honour then lowered the massive jewelled crown of state onto his head as the archbishop pronounced the act of coronation, and Richard became the King of England.

A solemn Mass was then celebrated while the new king sat on his throne for the first time, then the procession reformed with Richard at its head, carrying the royal sword in one hand and a jewelled sceptre in the other. It progressed to the west door, then turned and walked back solemnly to the quire, where it dispersed in a pre-arranged order. Richard left by way of the side door that led, through the old cloisters, to the side entrance to the palace, where a massive banquet was awaiting the invited guests whose contributions to the Crusade fund had earned them a seat.

An hour later the banquet was in full swing — with William and Adele seated at a table immediately behind the royal party, so Adele could be on hand should Eleanor require her — when there was a loud commotion on the other side of the closed double entrance doors to Westminster Hall. A liveried usher left his post just inside the doors and hurried down to the royal table, where he spoke urgently to the Lord High Constable, Henry de Bohun, Earl of Hereford, who was seated on the extreme left. His face reflected his concern as he rose and made his way towards Richard, who inclined his head downwards to receive the urgent message, then said something to Eleanor that caused them both to rise quickly from the table and make their way through the private door to the rear.

Adele rose and followed, in case her mistress might require her, but returned only moments later. 'It would be best to remain here, I think, since outside is all turmoil,' she told William.

'What's happened?' William asked.

She shuddered. 'Some Jews arrived with gifts, and the palace guards set about them. One of them was killed, and seemingly, when word got out, there were riots in the lower city, and houses were burned to the ground. There is a fear that the tumult will spread, and men at arms from the Tower have been dispersed to deal with it.'

V

The bubbling crucible of resentment that had been building against Jewish people living in England had finally broken the surface, and from a political perspective it could not have occurred at a worse time, on the very day of Richard's coronation.

For one thing, the Jews were often assumed to be rich, although this was a huge generalisation. They were also rumoured to have been highly favoured by successive Kings of England ever since they had arrived from Rouen during the reign of William the Conqueror, even though their rights and opportunities were originally very restricted. They were permitted to work as moneylenders — an occupation that was not prohibited by their religion but was condemned as 'usury' by the Catholic Church — and their earnings were heavily taxed, directly benefitting the monarch. The result was that many merchants in London, shipbuilders in Bristol and Portsmouth, weavers in Norwich and nobles at court owed money to Jewish dealers.

The non-Jews who worked in poorly paid and dangerous occupations resented the alleged wealth and seemingly favoured status of the Jewish communities in the larger towns, of which London and York were the prime examples. It was not long before this hostility was translated into vile and baseless rumours regarding their lifestyles. They were alleged to worship according to secret and sacred rites that gave them direct access to the Devil himself, during which they sacrificed their young in exchange for wealth. They were said to be unhygienic spreaders of pestilence who preyed upon unsuspecting Christian children and dragged them away to be sacrificed to their heathen gods. But above all, they were said to be protected by kings from any accusation of wrongdoing in exchange for vast loans of money.

On the day of Richard's coronation, two wealthy merchants from York had travelled south in order to present him with gifts from their community to express their delight at his accession, and to wish him long life and good health. They got as far as the public entrance to the Great Hall of Westminster, where they were halted by men at arms of the Palace Guard. A loud and acrimonious argument developed when the gentlemen from York were denied access to the Hall, and the guards reviled them with insulting epithets for members of their race. One of the merchants was sufficiently incensed to land a punch on the nose of one of the men at arms, who needed no further excuse to attack the hopelessly outnumbered and unarmed visitors. They were stripped naked, flogged with the staffs of their halberds and thrown out into the street.

Within the hour, rumours were spreading around the cramped streets of the old city to the east of Westminster. It was said that the newly crowned king had ordered, as his very first command, that every Jew in England be put to death. This was enough justification for the mob rule that followed, as Jewish families were hauled out into the streets to be brutally beaten to death while their houses were burned and their worldly goods scattered and stolen. Men at arms from the Tower of London were ordered to suppress seething riots in areas such as Newgate, St Paul's, Smithfield and Poultry, and the final death toll — all of the victims being Jewish — ran into double figures.

It was several hours before those attending the coronation banquet were told that it was once again safe to venture outside in order to take private barges or public wherries from Westminster Stairs. William and Adele, however, only needed to climb a few flights of stairs to reach the safety of their chambers.

Richard summoned William to the Audience Chamber two days later, and he presented himself with some apprehension.

The king waved him into a chair alongside him and called for wine to be served. He then turned to William with a smile. 'I have to congratulate you on your recent handling of that dreadful violation matter — the four Italian seafarers? They tell me that they were hung a few days before my coronation.'

'It was the jury that decided their guilt, sire,' William reminded him. 'Once they had been adjudged guilty, I had no option but to order their deaths, as prescribed by law.'

'A law that you yourself devised, or so my mother advises me. Did you leave no leeway in that law for the person sitting in judgment to influence the outcome?'

'Again, if I might with respect remind you, sire,' William insisted, 'the ones sitting in judgment are those called to serve as jurymen. They reach their decision entirely on what they hear from the witnesses.'

'And who determines what the witnesses are called to say?' Richard asked. 'And if it comes to that, whose is the decision regarding which witnesses to call?'

'That is the function of the sheriff, sire — either he or his bailiff. They enquire into the matter when it is reported, and they decide whose words the jury shall hear.'

'So the judge has no influence at all in the matter?'

'That is perhaps putting it too simply, sire. The judge is often called to rule upon what the witnesses are to be allowed to say. For example, if a witness is attempting to relay what someone *else* told them, then such "hearsay", as we call it, is ruled out, and the original observer is called to tell what they saw or heard for themself.'

'And who decides what charge shall be brought?'

'The sheriff, sire, when the case is first heard by what we call a "jury of presentment", who are in effect a body of men drawn from the place in which the crime is alleged to have been committed. They advise on what is alleged to have transpired. It is on that basis that the sheriff then draws up what is called an "indictment" against the person accused, basing his choice of charge on the facts that have been presented.'

Richard was thinking hard as he swirled his wine in his goblet. 'Let me pose you a particular, William. Say a man is accused of stealing a pig from another, but the facts only suggest that he bought that pig from a third person, but knew that this third person had himself stolen it. Would that first man — the one found in possession of the pig — be guilty of theft?'

'No, sire. He would be guilty only of having received the pig, knowing it to have been stolen. That is a different offence, and would ordinarily result only in a fine or a whipping in the stocks. Were it theft, the man's hand would be forfeit.'

'So answer me this,' Richard persisted. 'If the sheriff had sent the man to trial by a jury, charged with theft, when the facts only suggested that lesser offence, would you — as the judge at the trial — have the authority to amend the charge?'

'Not only the authority, sire — the sworn duty to do so.'

Richard sat back with a gentle nod. 'As I believed to be the case. So, let me pose you another imaginary situation. A man burns down the house of another, and the person residing in the house dies as a consequence. If the intention of the man who set the flame was solely that the house should burn, would he be guilty of the murder of the man inside it?'

'That question is worthy of one of our professors at Oxford, where many a debate among students has such a theme. But I suspect that you are not seeking to engage me purely in an exchange of metaphysics. You refer to those disgraceful scenes in the old city, do you not, when many Jewish people were killed?'

'I wish you to preside at the trials of those taken up by the constables on the orders of the Tower guard, William, and I wish those who are to stand trial to be accused only of the setting of the fire, and not of the "murders" of those who died in consequence.'

William was both shocked and sickened by what was being asked of him, but his legal brain was still functioning. 'If I judge your intentions aright, sire, then you must know that those same men would by law hang just as readily for what we call "fire-setting" as they would for murder.'

'Do not presume to judge my intentions, now or at any time in the future!' Richard yelled, then softened his manner as he saw William recoil from him in alarm. 'What I mean to say, William, is that it is of critical importance that the matter be approached cautiously by one who is best placed, by virtue of his legal wisdom, to ensure that the correct message is sent to the world at large by the outcome of the trial.'

'What message do you wish conveyed?' William asked coldly.

Richard had a carefully prepared justification for what he was requesting. 'It is important that justice is publicly visited on those whose rash actions resulted in innocent deaths. But it is equally important that those deaths not be categorised as murder.'

'Might I ask the reason for that, sire, since you are clearly entrusting me with the task?'

'You may. I do not wish it voiced abroad that those unfortunate wretches died because they were of the Jewish faith. It would only serve to encourage others.'

'Not if those responsible finish up on the gallows,' William argued.

Again, Richard appeared to be controlling the urge to yell as he took a deep breath and lowered his voice. 'My concern is that others may be inspired by what took place to seek further deaths among the Jewish community. We must seek to emphasise only the wickedness of setting fires, not the desire of Englishmen of any rank to see Jews exterminated.'

Richard's use of the word 'rank' alerted William to the real reason for this conversation, and he asked tentatively, 'Is it being rumoured that this might have been the case, and that perhaps persons of a certain "rank" may have been its real instigators?'

Richard sighed and nodded. 'There are some who have put it about that I ordered all Jews in England to be slaughtered. I hope that you at least cannot believe that to be true, but unfortunately I may also be said to have benefitted by the death of at least one of those who were killed.'

William settled for raised eyebrows, rather than asking the question directly.

Richard reluctantly added, in muted tones, 'A man named Aaron Geller, a diamond merchant who lived in Smithfield with his wife and two sons, all now dead. I borrowed five hundred pounds from him some months ago, in order to fund my Crusade. It was one of those agreements done only on a shake of the hand, by arrangement with the chancellor, and there will be no written record of the debt, since Aaron did not wish it to be known that he had helped to finance a Christian campaign in the Holy Land.'

William nodded. 'Now I understand, although I assume that Chancellor de Longchamp has been bidden to maintain his silence in the matter?'

'He needed no bidding, since he is one of my most loyal officials. I hope that I can also rely on your discretion in the matter?'

'You may,' William confirmed tersely, 'because those responsible will, if found guilty, hang anyway, and my conscience will not be strained. But it shall be as you wish, and the charges will be only those of fire-setting. We were lucky that no more houses caught alight, given the tightness of the dwellings in the old city.'

'You are also fortunate that your delicate conscience allowed you to comply with my wishes, William,' Richard replied ominously. 'You will recall the fate of Archbishop Becket?'

Whether or not it was a veiled threat, William left the audience feeling decidedly uncomfortable.

'Why should I pay in order to promote your likely death?' William demanded of his older son Hugh several days later, when he presented himself in his father's office chamber.

Hugh pouted in the self-justifying way that seemed to be second nature to him now that he enjoyed both the king's confidences and his daily company in the exercise yard to the side of the armoury. 'If I don't have the necessary battle equipment, I almost certainly *will* be killed,' he replied truculently. 'I need a new courser, because Ben's getting too old for the charge with a fully armed knight in his saddle. I can't afford a destrier, and in any case they're really only fit for tourneys — in desert sand you're better off with a lighter, faster mount.'

'Presumably you won't be charging into battle without suitable weaponry?' William asked resignedly. 'Will you need a new sword, shield, axe, lance, or what?'

'All of those, depending on our chosen battle tactic,' Hugh replied, unaware of any intended sarcasm. 'But when I return, I will be laden with spices, precious gems, rich carpets and all the other splendid luxuries. Then I can repay you.'

'You will repay your mother and myself simply by returning alive,' William replied gloomily. 'God forbid that we lose our first born in the service of a king who has not been on the throne for more than a few weeks.'

'I serve Richard only in the order of battle,' Hugh replied pompously. 'The true leader of this Crusade is God, and His agent is his Holiness the Pope. I shall be fighting for the very survival of the greatest icon of Christianity — the city of Jerusalem.'

'Remind me to inscribe that on your tombstone,' William grimaced. 'When do you depart?'

Hugh shrugged. 'We must await good weather in order to cross the Channel, and then hopefully we can enjoy the summer months in our journey south to a port from which to take ship for the Holy Land. Given what is said to be the fierce heat in Outremer, it would be better to arrive there once the winter has commenced. So, taking into account all those considerations, we anticipate departing London in April or May of the coming year. Mother will be some months ahead of us, or so it is rumoured.'

William's jaw dropped in alarm. 'Your mother is going on *Crusade?*'

'I'm not entirely sure that is the case,' Hugh said hastily. 'But I thought you would know that she is due to accompany Queen Eleanor wherever she is bound, and that she will be crossing the Channel ahead of us. Did Mother not tell you?'

'I knew nothing of this,' William replied, his face drained of colour. 'Perhaps she did not know herself. Surely the queen has other ladies? Your mother is hardly in the first bloom of youth.'

'You are probably correct,' Hugh sought to reassure him, even though he had already seen the documents outlining the order of departure and authorising the commission of the necessary vessels. 'But regarding the finance I require?'

'Did you doubt that it would be made available to you?' William asked. 'Just come back alive, is all I ask. And bring your mother with you, if she is foolhardy enough to follow the queen in her unwisdom.'

William lost no time in hastening up the stairs to their private chambers and tasking Adele with what Hugh had just revealed.

'It has not yet been finally decided,' Adele offered. 'It's not just Her Majesty, anyway. We shall be taking the Princess Alys with us.'

'Why, and where to?' William demanded.

Adele shook her head. 'We have not been advised. Eleanor is keeping matters very close, although there is a suggestion that we may venture south into Spain. At least, we have been advised to commission the lightest of clothing, so wherever we are truly bound is somewhere hot.'

'Pray God it is not the Holy Land,' William muttered. 'Perhaps Richard intends to marry Alys at long last, and wishes to do so in his native Aquitaine.'

Adele looked uncertainly back at him. 'I doubt that, else we ladies would have been instructed to commission gowns suitable for a wedding celebration. And Alys has been kept confined all these years, most recently in Winchester. She is more like a prisoner than a bride-to-be.'

'How many ladies will be in Eleanor's entourage, and why must it include you?' William demanded.

'You are also in the royal service, William — since when were we consulted in *any* matter, until something was required of us?'

William nodded grimly. 'Perhaps I should have followed my brother into the Church.'

'Then you would not have had me, and would not be the father of three children who you adore,' Adele reminded him.

He nodded again and drew her to him in a warm embrace. 'I just hope that at least one of my family remains alive at the end of all this upheaval,' he whispered hoarsely as he fought back the tears. 'Being in the royal service is as much a curse as a blessing these days.'

VI

Adele was seated in the captain's cabin at the stern of the *Kentish Rose* as it bucketed through a rising westerly swell on the short journey across the Channel to Boulogne. She was struggling with one of the most profound depressions she had ever experienced. On the padded bench alongside her was her mistress, Queen Dowager Eleanor, now a stately dame approaching seventy years of age, but lacking none of her former courtly charm as she pretended to listen attentively to the incessant prattle of Captain Francis Bartholomew. He was so honoured to have such a royal guest on board that it seemed that he might expire from lack of breath in his eagerness to be hospitable.

Seated in the far corner was Princess Alys of France, accompanied as always by a stern-faced man at arms drawn from her private guard in Winchester Castle, from which she had recently been transferred. She was now aged nineteen, unmarried, and no doubt wondering why she was being taken back — hopefully — to the land of her birth. Her intended husband, Richard of England, was seemingly in no hurry to share a marital bed with her, and she was secretly hoping that her half-brother King Philip had persuaded Richard to honour the Treaty of Montmirail reached between their respective fathers ten years previously. But when she'd made enquiry of her surly escort on the way to Dover, she'd been bluntly told, in a tone of voice that did not encourage further enquiry, that Richard was remaining in England for the time being.

The source of Adele's depression was twofold. First of all, there had been the usual tearful farewell on the quayside at

Dover — the hugs, kisses, endearments and promises that seemed to be a regular penance for those who served a court that travelled constantly back and forth across the Channel. But this time it was different, since Adele and William had even less idea than usual when they might be reunited, or even where Adele was bound. Queen Eleanor had remained tight-lipped regarding their destination, revealing only that it would initially involve Normandy, but with a clear implication that they would be travelling beyond that. Only the fact that Richard remained in London was some sort of vague reassurance that they were not themselves embarking on the long-heralded Crusade. At least, not yet.

When they docked in Boulogne, there was a large contingent of men at arms awaiting them. Their chainmail was draped with the emblazoned surcoats of two gold lions passant on a red background that denoted them as serving the House of Normandy, which was also — at least for the moment — the House of Plantagenet and England. A litter awaited Queen Eleanor, with two docile palfreys for Adele and Alys, who were to ride on either side of the litter.

The party reached Rouen on the third day, having been accommodated overnight in noble houses in Abbeville and Neufchatel. No sooner had they arrived than Adele received a message from Eleanor, conveyed by one of the palace ushers, that she was not to unpack more of her clothing than she needed for two nights, and that Eleanor wished her to attend upon her immediately.

Expecting to be asked to assist with one of the queen's elegant but complicated head coverings, Adele was surprised to be offered a seat and a goblet of the local *vin de pays*.

'You received my message, clearly,' Eleanor said, 'and no doubt you are now wondering why we shall not be biding long here in Rouen?'

'It is not my place to question, madam,' Adele replied demurely, hoping nevertheless that she was about to learn where they were headed.

'We are here mainly in order to leave the Lady Alys in a secure place. Once I am satisfied that she is suitably accommodated, we shall be journeying to Poitiers, from there to Aquitaine, and then on through Gascony and across the mountains into Castile, where my daughter Eleanor rules as queen alongside her husband Alfonso.'

'It has been many years since you last saw your daughter?' Adele asked politely.

Eleanor nodded. 'Not since she left us at the tender age of twelve, in order to be married to a youth of seventeen. I protested, but King Henry was anxious to reinforce our borders across the Pyrenees. Eleanor is now approaching twenty years of age, and has given me three granddaughters who I have yet to meet.'

'I must admit, as the mother of a daughter myself,' Adele replied tactfully, 'that I was always fearful that she might be married off at too young an age for childbearing. It is said that one's inner workings as a woman can be damaged beyond repair by such a process. Is that perhaps why the marriage between your son Richard and the Princess Alys of France has been delayed these many years?'

Eleanor looked hard into Adele's face, then smiled. 'You are as skilled as your husband when it comes to enquiring into a matter with diplomacy and discretion. Can you keep a secret?'

'I hope you know me well enough by now not to need to enquire,' Adele replied.

'Indeed I do, and please accept my apology. But what I have to disclose must be treated with the utmost discretion and secrecy. I only mention it now because you made enquiry, and because I shall require your assistance in due course.'

Adele remained tactfully silent.

Eleanor fixed her gaze on the far wall of the chamber and spoke without making eye contact. 'Alys will be remaining here, and hopefully her brother will believe that she is awaiting her bridegroom. But the truth is that she will not be marrying Richard. Before you enquire, there is no proof of the wicked rumour that my late husband took her virtue, so that is not the reason why the former treaty will not be honoured. But whatever the reason, King Philip must not learn of the true state of affairs, since Richard is relying on him being by his side when they embark on the long-delayed Crusade.'

'Richard's heart lies elsewhere?' Adele asked.

Eleanor grinned. '*That* rumour is also without truth, in case you were wondering. My son does not prefer the company of men, except on the field of battle. As to where his heart may lie, I care not, but it is my ambition that his boots shall lie in Navarre.'

When Adele looked perplexed, Eleanor explained further.

'Navarre is a kingdom beyond the Pyrenees, currently ruled by King Sancho. It lies between Gascony and Castile, and an alliance with its king would be of inestimable value to our possessions in the south-west. There has been a tradition of hostilities between Navarre and Castile that I fear may re-open, thereby putting my daughter Eleanor in peril. And if Castile were to fall to Navarre, then we would have no ally to attack Navarre's other borders should Sancho turn his attentions to Gascony. So you see the strategic importance of Navarre to Richard's empire?'

'I believe so,' Adele replied, although her mind was reeling. One thing, however, had become abundantly clear, and she ventured to ask, 'Does this King Sancho by any chance have a daughter of marriageable age?'

'He has two, the older of whom is called Berengaria. She is fourteen years of age, and is proclaimed by those who know her to be beautiful, both in appearance and in temperament. Richard has yet to set eyes upon her, but he will do as he is told in the matter. In short, Adele, we shall be journeying at length into Navarre, although we shall do so circumspectly, in order that none — least of all Philip of France — may become aware of our true intent. Now, answer me this. Should we succeed in securing Berengaria as a bride for Richard, is there some lady among those who attend me who you consider would be a suitable senior lady for a young princess of Navarre?'

Adele thought briefly. 'There is Lady Edwina, madam. She is of Welsh stock, and her father Edmund is one of your Marcher lords, with estates in Flint. She is somewhat short in height and dark of colouring, so might well look appropriate alongside a princess from the south of your lands. You may have had cause to notice her during recent banquets, because she is wont to giggle excessively if approached by young noblemen.'

'Yes, a comely little thing, as I recall,' Eleanor agreed. 'She will do admirably, so please ensure that she travels with us when we move south.'

'When will that be, madam?'

'Whenever I am reassured that Alys is firmly isolated from any communication with her brother. That should not take long. Now, let us enquire if there is some of that excellent local soft cheese for supper.'

William was both angry and anxious. The Sheriff of London had manipulated the criminal proceedings following the murder of Jews in the city in such a way that William was left in little doubt that King Richard had been in his ear, threatening him with loss of office if anyone was convicted of murder. The charges presented against the five men taken up by the constables had therefore been restricted to the setting of fires.

William was well aware, from having spoken with some of these constables at length, that several Jews had been butchered in the street as they'd fled from their burning homes. However, the only deaths recorded on the presentments were those of families that had unwisely remained within their dwellings even when their roof timbers had begun to collapse, because they were fearful of the mob awaiting them outside.

It was equally obvious to William, sitting a full five feet above the well of the courtroom in the Great Hall of Westminster in order to control the proceedings, that certain witnesses whose evidence might have been vital to establishing that the majority of the deaths had been at the hands of a blood-lusting mob had not been cited or summoned. Instead, the few witnesses who *were* called spoke only of the actions of the five accused of setting fire to those dwellings in which entire families had perished. Even though the jury experienced little difficulty in entering findings of guilt, and William had felt no qualms about ordering that those responsible pay the ultimate penalty, he was sickened by the realisation that he had been manipulated and duped.

Three days later, he had forced himself to attend the executions in Smithfield, to which the condemned men were dragged through the dusty streets, barefoot and blindfolded, behind carts that were then employed as the platforms from which the men were 'launched into eternity' as the horses pulling them were prodded into moving forward. The jeers and catcalls of the mob rang hollowly in his ears; the men they were mocking unquestionably deserved death, but several others had escaped retribution for actions that had been even more direct and brutal.

The reason for William's anxiety was not that he might be accused of dereliction of duty; after all, he had done precisely what had been required of him. It was for the future of the criminal justice machinery that he had conceived and persuaded the late King Henry to establish. To judge by the experience of his first few weeks as Chief Justice, it was a system that could be manipulated and exploited to obtain whatever outcome one desired, provided that one was in a position of power and influence within it. He was at the very top of the justice tree, but seemingly powerless to prevent corruption by those beneath him, working at the level of enquiry and accusation. Sheriffs in particular seemed to enjoy unfettered discretion, and were clearly open to bribery or threat.

His mood was not improved when he received a visit from Justiciar de Longchamp, who first of all congratulated him on his 'success' in achieving the 'hoped-for' outcome of the trials. He then asked whether he intended to visit other areas of the nation in which it was anticipated that similar troubles might break the surface.

'Where did you have in mind?' William asked testily. 'And wherever that might be, will I be expected to "achieve the same outcome", as you put it? Save King Richard from any suggestion that he has in some way ordered the extermination of those to whom he owes money?'

De Longchamp slammed an angry fist down on the table between them. 'That is an outrageous slur upon a man who has raised us both to the positions that we occupy! I shall not report it to His Majesty, since he is shortly to depart on Crusade, doing his Christian duty. A man of great courage, great military might and deep religious conviction.'

'And, it would seem, with an urgent need to preserve his image while innocent families are slaughtered!' William spat back. 'Am I indeed to be the bringer of justice to the nation, as I had hoped when I accepted the position of Chief Justice, or am I simply a dog employed to bark at selected intruders?'

De Longchamp's eyes narrowed. 'You are entrusted with dispensing justice, certainly, but as you must realise there are many different opinions regarding what constitutes justice. I hope that you bear that in mind when you journey north.'

'To where, exactly?'

'There have been ugly incidents in parts of the Eastern counties,' de Longchamp replied. 'Most notably Norwich, Stamford and Lincoln, and there is said to be a rising tide of unrest in York. The sheriffs in each of these places appear to have either ignored the pleas of those whose family members have perished, or sought to cast blame on common criminals, such as robbers. The result has been that those who are believed to have been behind the deaths of prominent Jewish merchants — those who owed them considerable sums of money — have not only escaped punishment, but have also let it be rumoured that the deaths were ordered by our master King Richard. This clearly cannot be allowed to continue.'

'So you wish me to travel north for long enough to once again preserve the king's reputation, regardless of where the justice lies?'

'The king was *not* behind these deaths!' de Longchamp yelled in William's face. 'Those who serve him would best do so by nailing the lie on notices outside every church in the land! Or, in your case, unearthing the truth and holding those responsible to account, while removing from office the wicked sheriffs who have allowed this sorry state of affairs to continue. Now, when do you intend to leave?'

William took several deep breaths before responding. 'As you will know, my estate lies well to the north of here, slightly to the west of Nottingham. I propose to visit it in order to assure myself that all is well there; then I might consider travelling east in order to investigate what has occurred, although it is probably too late to restore any vestige of justice to those matters. I shall report back to you in due course, although should I do so with honesty regarding what I discover, it may not be to your liking.'

De Longchamp's face softened. 'I trust you to report back faithfully, William, and my only concern is that King Richard be not unjustly accused of something of which he is innocent. Surely you share that concern?'

'My primary concern lies in securing the conviction and punishment of the guilty,' William replied coldly, 'regardless of who they may be. Now, if you would excuse me, I must make urgent preparations for my departure.'

A week later, accompanied by the two men at arms from his office who rode with him everywhere to ensure his safety, William turned into the southern approach to his Repton estate from the track that ran along the north bank of the fast flowing Trent. The manor house lay almost a mile inside the wide acres interspersed with timber copses, and he smiled at the prospect of spending a few days among friendly faces, and enquiring as to the progress of his younger son Robert. In particular he hoped that his education was progressing well under the supervision of the sub-prior of the local holy house, and that before long he would begin to both talk and deport himself as befitted the son of a royal official, rather than a farmhand.

He saw movement up ahead to his left, where two figures were moving swiftly towards the Manor Wood, from which much of the timber was felled for onward transport to Swarkestone Mill. With a smile he recognised the tall, young man in the lead as his son Robert, then reminded himself that Robert ought to have been at his lessons in the priory. Transferring his gaze to the person who Robert was all but dragging behind him, he realised that it was a young woman of some fifteen or sixteen years of age. She was dressed like a serving girl or land labourer, in a simple smock that should have been covered by a kirtle, given the cold weather.

He ordered his escort to rein in their mounts, then did the same and raised himself in the saddle so as to be more visible. Then he called loudly and waved until Robert became aware of their presence, and said something to the girl. They both struck out across the rough grass in William's direction, and he marvelled yet again at the height and seemingly robust health of a boy who had barely attained his sixteenth year.

When the couple reached the trio on horseback, Robert cast a cursory glance at William's companions and asked, 'Ay up then, Dad — are yer 'ere ter arrest me?'

William frowned with distaste. 'Has your spoken English not improved one jot since I began paying the priory to correct it? Try again.'

Robert grinned. 'Good morning, Father. Are you here to secure my arrest?'

'That's better,' William said, 'and I might be, if your speech doesn't improve.'

'I can do it either way,' Robert assured him, 'but I wouldn't get much respect from the estate workers if I sounded like you. Oh ... sorry, what I meant was ... well...'

'I know what you meant,' William chuckled. 'Now, are you going to introduce us to the young lady?'

'You've met her already,' Robert told him as his face suddenly reddened. 'She's my sister, Beth — or at least, she was until you told me that you're my father. Now she's just a friend.'

There was a faint snort from one of the men at arms, and William asked, 'A friend who you were dragging into the Manor Wood?'

'We was just checkin' the trees,' Beth replied defensively.

This time the man at arms burst out laughing, until silenced by an irritated look from William. He turned back to the couple and asked, 'And are they still there?'

'What Beth means,' Robert hastened to clarify, 'is that we think we might be able to fill an order from the mill at Swarkestone. They need oaks of at least fifteen feet in height, for the reinforcement of the bridge over the Trent. They're paying a top rate for every foot of oak that goes to that height, and we were just going into the wood to count how many we might have that we can fell.'

'It sounds as if the estate is thriving under your management,' William said.

Robert's face fell. 'That's not quite correct, Father, I'm afraid. At least, we're managing well for ourselves, but it was a very bad harvest last year, and that hard winter has held back the spring sowing. The tenants weren't able to pay the Martinmas or Candlemas rents, and there's doubt regarding the upcoming Whitsunday payments, so the estate revenues are seriously diminished.'

'I hope you didn't evict anyone.'

Robert shook his head. 'Of course not — we're better Christians than that, and Father Christopher, the prior of Repton, reminded us of our charitable duty to those less fortunate than ourselves. But lots of the local lords have been evicting for months now. I'm surprised you weren't set upon by robbers on your way here.'

'With two heavily armed men riding alongside me?' William asked.

'You wouldn't be the first. Seems that the Bishop of Lincoln was set upon as he rode through the Shire Wood, north of Nottingham. A bunch of ruffians took his gold, his donkey and even his vestments, leaving him naked and battered at the side of the road. The local sheriff's put a price on the heads of those responsible.'

'Well, we're here anyway,' William said, 'and we could benefit from some warm stew and a pot or two of ale. Is your father still alive, Beth?'

'O' course,' Beth replied as she moved from Robert's side and began to walk up the gentle slope that led to the manor house. 'So's me mam. The fresh bread should be out've the oven be the time we gets up ter the 'ouse, so foller me.'

An hour later, his escort having been fed in the kitchen and shown to their quarters above the stables, William sat to the side of the fireplace in the Hall with his estate steward, Thomas Derby, on the other side. They both drank mulled wine and ate lumps of cheese and warm, fresh bread.

'Robert tells me that last year's harvest was bad,' William began.

Thomas nodded. 'Did he also tell yer that we allowed the tenants ter keep their cottages? I 'opes yer doesn't mind, only it's bin no better anywhere else, they tell me, so it's not their fault.'

'No, you did exactly what I would have done,' William assured him, 'and I'm more than happy to leave matters in your hands, since my duties keep me away from here most of the time.'

Thomas looked relieved. 'The countess's also kept busy? Is that why she's not wiv yer this time?'

'Yes, she's journeyed across the Channel with Queen Dowager Eleanor. I just hope that King Richard doesn't take them with him to the Holy Land.'

'Two women? Surely not?'

'It is to be hoped not, anyway. But she will be delighted when I eventually get to advise her what a splendid young man Robert's turning out to be, thanks to your supervision. Although I was a little concerned to find him heading for the Manor Wood with your daughter Beth, rather than attending to his studies.'

'They doesn't mean no 'arm,' Thomas hastened to reassure him. 'Them's more like brother an' sister, the way things worked out, an' yer know what young folks is like.'

'I was referring more to his absence from the priory,' William said, now firmly convinced that Robert and Beth saw themselves rather differently than did most brothers and sisters.

'The sub-prior what teaches 'im went down wiv an ague a couple've weeks back,' Thomas told him, 'and we kept 'im away from the priory, rather than risk all've us gettin' it an' all.'

'Quite right too,' William agreed. 'But what was all this Robert was telling me about robbers on the public highway? We get them on the roads approaching London, obviously, because that's where their wealthier marks are likely to be travelling, but here in Derbyshire?'

Thomas nodded sadly. 'It's the same everywhere yer goes, these days. The landlords took ter throwin' their tenants off the land when they couldn't pay their rents, an' now they're livin' in the woods an' waylayin' travellers in order ter rob 'em. There's a real bad bunch've 'em livin' in the Shire Wood, they reckons. That's just north o' Nottinum, an' the road ter York goes through it, so lots've travellers use it.'

'Robert mentioned those to me when I first arrived. What's the sheriff doing about them?' William asked.

Thomas made a faint snorting noise. 'Nowt, as usual. All 'e spends 'is time doin' is suckin' up ter them what lives in the castle, chasin' folks what steals the king's venison in the Shire Wood, an' 'angin' 'em at the crossroads at Ollerton. Me brother lives up by Edwinstowe, an' 'e tells me that there's nary a day goes by wivout somebody or other bein' caught by the royal verderers an' 'anded over ter the constables ter be 'ung. That's if they're lucky — some've 'em's bin slow-cooked over a fire! It's got ser bad that I've forbidden Beth ter visit 'er favourite cousin Alice, what wiv robbers 'idin' in the trees an' verderers lookin' fer folks ter accuse o' things they ain't done.'

William frowned. 'If there are injustices being committed, then perhaps I can use my official position to prevent them.'

Thomas gave a hollow laugh. 'Good luck wiv that. But talkin' o' Beth, yer should know that Robert's taken ter travellin' wiv 'er wherever she goes. She's a big girl now, o' course, an' some've the lads from the village sometimes does an' says rude things to 'er, so Robert chases 'em off. 'Ope yer doesn't mind, but I thought yer should know what a good an' noble lad 'e's turned inter.'

'You don't think that he might perhaps be jealous of other young men paying her attention?'

'What, 'is own sister? Surely not?'

William opted not to pursue the point, but began enquiring about the state of the estate finances, and plans for stock-rearing and timber-felling and suchlike.

VII

For the next few days, William allowed Robert — usually with Beth a few feet behind — to show him around the wide acreage and impress him with his management of the large estate. On the fourth day he was resting by the fireplace ahead of supper when Thomas entered the Hall, interrupting William's musings as to where Adele might be now, travelling with Eleanor.

'There's some bloke from the town ter see yer,' Thomas told William. There was a tall man behind him, armed with a huge club hanging from his belt.

'I'm Constable Applegarth, beggin' yer pardon an' all, yer lordship. Only yer wanted at the castle.'

'*Nottingham* Castle?' William asked.

Applegarth nodded. 'Yeah, Prince John wants ter see yer — it's urgent.'

'Prince John's in residence at the castle?' William asked unnecessarily. 'Why am I summoned to see *him*? If it's a law and order matter, why not the sheriff?'

'Sheriff de Lacy's gone ter Lunnun, ter join the Crusade, yer lordship. But we 'ad word that yer was back on yer estate, an' Prince John needs yer ter travel north. Seems as though there's bin some more Jews killed in York, an' the place's in a state've chaos, they reckons.'

Later that day, William, accompanied by his two men at arms, and with Constable Applegarth to confirm his identity to the four guards on duty at the wooden gatehouse, passed through the outer bailey of Nottingham Castle and up the steep slope that gave entry to the middle bailey. Three more men at arms brought their halberds upright, signalling that they could pass through the gate cut into the massive wall. They were finally in the upper bailey, where they dismounted and announced their business to a further set of men at arms, this time wearing tunics emblazoned with the royal emblem of golden lions passant on a red background.

They were met inside the entrance hall by a dour-faced middle-aged man who, to judge by his dress, had only just arrived himself, given the wet mud that still clung to his riding boots. He gave the briefest of bows in William's direction before addressing him. 'I am William de Wendenal, High Sheriff of Nottinghamshire, Derbyshire and the Royal Forests. The prince awaits us.'

'I thought the local sheriff was away on the Crusade,' William said.

The man smiled frostily. 'Roger de Lacy is now the *former* sheriff. We cannot leave the safety of two counties in the hands of an absentee, nor can we allow outlawed peasants turned cut-throats to roam the Shire Wood to our north. Therefore, in his generosity and out of concern for the safety of this portion of his realm, Prince John appointed me to fill the vacant office. Now, shall we proceed without further delay? The matter is said to be urgent.'

They mounted the broad staircase that led to the Great Hall, at the far end of which a huge fire was blazing, even though they were well into early summer. A small, richly robed man with a haunted facial expression sat in a padded chair three times too large for him, sipping wine from a jewelled goblet and staring into the fire. He half turned to acknowledge their entrance once it was announced by the liveried usher, and William got his second view of the king's younger brother John, this time from the front. It was not impressive.

'You are the Chief Justice of England appointed by my brother Richard?' John asked, and when William confirmed this, giving a half bow, the prince's face darkened. 'I want you to journey to York without delay, there to hang those responsible for this latest outrage provoked by my brother's greed and indifference to the safety of the nation he was unwisely bequeathed by our father on his deathbed.'

'I shall of course do as you wish, my lord…' William began, only to be halted by a hand held high in the air.

'You will address me as "Your Majesty", and you will regard what I ask of you as a *command*, not a wish.'

'Even then,' William replied coldly, angered by the arrogant rebuke, 'I shall need to be advised of the nature of the outrage, and the reason for my urgent departure north.'

'Jews,' John replied. 'Jews slaughtered as the result of my brother's secret instructions to his misguided followers up north.'

William was not sure how to respond to such a blatant condemnation of King Richard. His hesitation clearly irritated the little man in the padded chair, who raised both eyebrows mockingly and sneered, 'No doubt he sought to assure you of his innocence of those deaths in London? Not to mention similar deaths in Lincoln and Norwich?'

'The deaths in London were the result of rash actions by men inflamed by liquor and jealous of the wealth of their neighbours, who happened to be Jewish,' William started to explain, but he realised from the stony expression on John's face that he was wasting his breath. Nevertheless, he persevered. 'His Majesty *did* express his concern that those ill-disposed towards him had started rumours of his involvement in the deaths, which he was alleged to have ordered because of the unfortunate coincidence that he had recently secured a loan from one of those who were killed...'

A raised hand once again commanded silence, and another sneer followed as John replied, 'You will find, should you take the trouble to enquire, that those who died in both Lincoln and Norwich had also loaned money to nobles seeking to equip themselves to follow my brother on his lack-witted enterprise in the Holy Land. The land of England has never been in more dire need of a firm royal hand, and what does the idiot do? Pawn the royal jewels, empty the Treasury and take himself off at the whim of a Pope whose very right to occupy his throne in Rome is currently being challenged. It has fallen to those who truly love England to ensure that it does not sink into a mire of starvation, lawlessness and anarchy. Do you disagree with that? If so, then the justice system will be the first casualty in all this.'

'I am obviously committed to maintaining peace within the realm,' William retorted, 'else your brother would not have appointed me.'

'Really? His inability to choose the right people for the important offices of the nation was clearly demonstrated by his appointment, as Justiciar, of that cretin de Longchamp, who by all accounts paid for his position. Did you by any chance pay for your current office?'

'Most certainly not!' William replied hotly. His eyes met John's in silent challenge.

The prince gave him a chilling smile. 'In that case, you will lose no time in journeying to York, hanging a few murderers and returning to me with confirmation that they were inspired by the man who calls himself the King of England. You are excused the presence.'

As they walked back down the hallway to the staircase, Sheriff de Wendenal seemed amused by the black look on

William's face. However, he opted to take advantage of the man's obvious devastation at John's curt treatment of him.

'No need to take it personally, friend,' he told William. 'His Majesty is in an ill humour of late, due to his inability to go hunting.'

'Why not?' William asked out of sullen politeness. 'The weather has been fine enough, and the beasts are plentiful on my estate, so why not others?'

'There are no beasts left in the Shire Wood to the north of here, where Prince John likes to hunt,' de Wendenal explained. 'He has a hunting lodge at Clipstone, in the heart of the "Royal Forest", as we call that part of the Shire Wood, and it was previously well stocked with deer and other game. But since the evictions in the county, those dispossessed have formed themselves into small bands and begun hunting the royal deer, in order to drag their carcases back to their lairs hidden deep in the wood. When the royal verderers catch them I have them hanged, or occasionally roasted, but that seems to have no effect. I have a list of more than a dozen who I've declared to be outlaws, with prices on all their heads, but no-one seems prepared to give them up when we ride through their villages, burning their thatch and flogging their wives and children.'

William was aghast, and turned his face angrily towards de Wendenal's as he halted, forcing the sheriff to do likewise. 'If I understand what you are telling me, all these troubles began because of what you called "evictions". What lawful cause led to those evictions?'

'They fell behind in their rents,' de Wendenal explained. 'Most of them are tenants of the Royal Forest, which is administered by me, as bailiff. On the order of Prince John I evicted those whose payments were in arrears, and they repaid me by poaching the royal deer, which is punishable by death.'

'The alternative would be death from starvation,' William pointed out. 'I have tenants on my own estate, but I foreswore evictions because that would not have been likely to improve matters for anyone. Better to await an improved harvest, and have the land properly cultivated by tenants whose gratitude for your charity makes them work all the harder.'

'These oafs do not understand charity,' de Wendenal replied heatedly, 'and neither does Prince John. A lease is a lease, and the peasants who withheld their rents were undermining royal authority. This clearly cannot be tolerated, and I have my instructions.'

'So the actions you have taken since your appointment, which must have been recent, have been on the authority of Prince John?'

'On his *orders*. When he first approached me with a view to my appointment, he secured from me a promise that I would leave no actions unperformed that he commanded. And so I do what must be done.'

'You realise that, by law, you hold office independently of any man's bidding — even a king's?' William challenged him.

De Wendenal gave a derisive snort. 'You have sampled but a small portion of the anger of which His Majesty is capable when thwarted. I have experienced worse, and would not wish to repeat it.'

'Then I feel sorry for you,' William replied sadly as they reached the entrance doors, and he called for his mount. 'I hope that this will be my only visit to this castle.'

'I was instructed to ensure that you return here with news of how things fare in York,' de Wendenal replied.

William frowned with displeasure as he swung into the saddle and urged his mount down the slope. As he rode back to Repton, deep in thought, he forced himself to think of

Adele, wondering where Eleanor had dragged her in her royal progress across the Channel.

The ladies occupying William's thoughts were already in Navarre, after a six-week progress across those principalities that were still firmly in Plantagenet hands. The three-day sojourn at Poitiers had allowed time for messengers to be dispatched south, and they had been graciously received in Gascony, before the tedious and somewhat hazardous crossing of the mountain range they called the Pyrenees. They were then lovingly welcomed to Castile, where Eleanor's second-born daughter, named after her, reigned as queen.

Diplomatic overtures had secured a safe crossing into Navarre, where they had been met by an escort from King Sancho on the second day of their journey, and guided to the capital town of Pamplona. Stately apartments had been prepared in anticipation of their arrival at the Olite Palace in which the king and queen lived in breath-taking luxury with their two daughters. The oldest of these, Berengaria, was to host the magnificent banquet for which Eleanor and Adele were preparing themselves when a richly liveried page tapped on their door and poked his head around it.

'Would you be prepared to receive the Princess Berengaria?' he asked in French that betrayed his Spanish origins.

Eleanor looked up in surprise. 'But of course!' she enthused. 'Please do not leave her waiting outside — grant her entry immediately!'

Adele got her first glimpse of the young woman that Eleanor had chosen as a more suitable bride for her warlike son, and all but gasped in amazement. It was almost as if Eleanor had commanded that a statue of one of the saintly women of history be removed from a cathedral and brought to life.

Berengaria was ravishingly beautiful in a 'Virgin Mary' sort of way, with angelic features that looked as if some accomplished sculptor had carved them lovingly out of alabaster. Her dark eyes shone like beacons from a fresh face free of any blemish, and her dark auburn hair was tinted with lighter golden strands that shimmered in the candlelight.

Berengaria walked slowly forward, then executed a perfect curtsey as she enquired, in French heavily accented with the local dialect, 'The husband, he is not yet here?'

'He is on his way from England,' Eleanor told her, 'and we are to meet him in Sicily.'

'When will we depart?' was the next eager question. 'I am anxious to set eyes on this man they say is so handsome and brave.'

Eleanor smiled with satisfaction. 'The stories you have heard do not do him full credit. But may I congratulate you on your excellent French?'

'I have learned it from my tutor, who is a holy brother from Bordeaux,' Berengaria explained. 'He also teaches me Latin, Greek, and the Holy Scriptures. This will be suitable for my wifely duties?'

There was a slightly embarrassed silence as Eleanor and Adele reminded themselves of what 'wifely duties' involved for the consort of an active, virile warrior, but Eleanor quickly recovered. 'Your father has clearly advised you of the purpose of our visit. Once the full terms of our treaty have been agreed, we shall depart for Sicily. You are prepared for travel?'

'I have had all my gowns packed and have been ready to depart for several days now,' Berengaria said. 'I am only too relieved to learn that my father was not deceiving me when he advised that a handsome and mighty king wished to take me for his wife. I only hope that he finds me pleasing. Now I must prepare for the banquet, if I might be excused?'

Eleanor nodded, and Berengaria gave another curtsey before gliding from the chamber on what seemed like hidden feet. Eleanor sat back with a sigh of satisfaction, and Adele ventured a question.

'*Will* your son find her pleasing, do you think?'

Eleanor replied with a hollow laugh. 'She is pleasing to me, so Richard will simply have to make the best of things.'

VIII

Hugh de Repton was only too glad to see the distant spires of Vézelay in central Burgundy. They had been journeying for ever, it seemed, and it was arguable whether the sea crossing had been the worst. Having heaved out of Dartmouth in a heavy spring gale and battled for three days against a persistent westerly swell, they'd finally moored in St Malo in Brittany, a fleet of over two dozen ships that between them carried a force of some eight hundred men and their horses.

The reason for the choice of such a westerly landfall had become obvious once they'd struck across land for day after miserable day, through Le Mans, Orleans and God alone knew how many small villages. Only after they'd put Orleans behind them had Richard chosen to reveal that their destination was the hilltop Abbey of Vézelay. Its high tower shimmered in the midday sun across the flat plain that they were crossing in order to reach this revered place of pilgrimage that boasted the relics of Mary Magdalene. Because of its spiritual significance, it had been the site of several Crusade proclamations, and was regarded as the perfect place from which to launch a holy war to regain Jerusalem for God while acquiring blessings from the bones of one of Christ's devoted followers. From a purely military point of view it was also a convenient midway point between the Channel and the Mediterranean ports, from which they could take ship for Acre or Tyre.

But they weren't heading for Vézelay simply for convenience, or even in search of a miracle from a set of ancient bones. They had agreed to meet there with the forces of King Philip of France, who together with Richard of

England would be leading the Third Crusade. To judge by the many pennants flying in the stiff breeze from almost every tall building in the approaching town, the French were already here, and it would be one of Hugh's tasks, as a senior member of Richard's immediate entourage, to ensure that English and French men at arms did not fight among themselves, rather than reserving their malice for the enemy.

Hugh was one of those grouped around Richard as they walked into the chapter house of the monastery attached to the abbey, where Philip of France awaited them with a small retinue of his own. The two monarchs embraced, and Philip took the belated opportunity to congratulate Richard on his coronation.

'It will be pleasing to visit my sister Alys once she is queen of your nation, which hopefully has now settled into a lengthy period of peace following the tumult of recent years,' he said in a tone of voice that was laced more with menace than sincerity.

'There is much to achieve elsewhere, before I may take my place as the monarch of a nation that has been blessed by God,' Richard replied diplomatically as he took the vacant seat without invitation, and nodded to the server that he was ready for a goblet of wine.

Philip looked him firmly in the eye. 'This will presumably entail yet another delay in your marriage to Alys, who I am advised is not travelling with you.'

'The Holy Land is no place for a woman, by all accounts,' Richard countered, 'least of all a woman of such delicacy and breeding as the Princess Alys. She is safely installed behind the walls of Rouen.'

'While you and your retinue travelled from St Malo by way of Le Mans and Orleans,' Philip observed. 'You were clearly not anxious to say your fond farewells on this side of *La Manche*.'

'We did so in Winchester, on my way to our port of Dartmouth, from which we set sail.'

'The same Winchester in which she was kept under close guard for several years, during which she was faithfully attended by your late father?' Philip asked stonily.

Hugh looked apprehensively at the French king's immediate guard in case they were reaching for their weapons. But the awkward moment passed as Richard asked, 'Which sea port should we favour for our departure, and which should be our port of destination in the Holy Land?'

Philip's brow creased in thought. 'I have over a thousand men and horses in my train, and you would seem to be accompanied by approximately the same number. There is not a single port on the southern coast that has sufficient vessels with the capacity to convey such a large army, so I propose that I travel to the Italian town of Genoa, there to take ship for Tyre. You may wish to have your fleet meet you in Marseille, then join me for my proposed siege of Acre.'

'I will need to send messengers to Bordeaux, where my fleet is currently moored, taking on fresh supplies,' Richard frowned. 'The delay may result in my late arrival across the Mediterranean to rejoin you.'

'I will await your fleet in Sicily, in order that we may undertake the final voyage together, thereafter sharing the glory of triumphing over the enemy,' Philip said. 'Now, let us give the order for dinner to be served, and we may idle away this pleasant afternoon in toasts to our joint success on Crusade, and the further tightening of our family ties with a marriage that has been too long delayed.'

Three months later, Richard was raging that his fleet had still not put into Marseille, but he was also refusing to spend valuable coinage on hiring another fleet locally. In the main, the vessels that they could see moored in the old port were built for fishing, and very few of them looked capable of transporting an army of men in their heavy armour, and the horses that would carry them into battle, across even an expanse of ocean as traditionally tranquil as the Mediterranean.

He held a council of war that Hugh attended, at which their options were considered one by one. Hugh and several others would have preferred to wait for their own fleet, if necessary sending scouts around the coast of Iberia in order to ascertain where it might have got to, but Richard was not in favour of that suggestion. He was clearly anxious to reach Sicily with the minimum delay, and he explained his reasons to Hugh and a selected handful of the seniors from his personal retinue as they sat in an alehouse overlooking the quayside, which was half full of fishing barques moored for the night.

'For one thing,' he began, 'I do not wish Philip to get there so far in advance of us that he empties the countryside of the supplies that we shall need to load ahead of our departure. Secondly, and more to the immediate point, my mother should be there by now, along with a very important travelling companion. And I'm not referring to *your* mother, Hugh. There will soon be a significant change in our relationship with Philip of France, and I do not wish it disclosed until we have retained his friendship and alliance for long enough to retake Acre.'

'Where in Sicily will your mother be lodged?' another of the retinue asked.

Richard smiled. 'With my sister Joan, who is queen consort to King William of Sicily. We may be assured of a warm welcome, and hopefully some additional funds in the form of fresh supplies for our ocean crossing. And once there we can either borrow ships from her, or send word that the fleet that brought us out from England is to continue down the Mediterranean to a suitable port, such as Messina. I therefore propose that we waste no more time in this stinking fish market, but head overland to Sicily.'

The groans that met this proposal were ignored as the necessary preparations were made, and the cavalcade set off, heading along the coastal shoreline through Toulon, Nice, Genoa, Pisa, Rome and Naples. The hot summer caused the death of several horses, provoked dozens of desertions and fermented general unrest among the bedraggled, stinking and exhausted men who remained loyal. They finally marched into Messina, on the north shore of Sicily, six weeks after their departure from Marseille.

Far from receiving the heroes' welcome they had anticipated, they found the town subdued, and the townsfolk tight-lipped. Hugh was left with the massive task of finding billets for all the English troops, an undertaking made all the more difficult by the fact that Philip's army was already here, having sailed gently down the Italian coast from Genoa. Richard lost no time in enquiring after his sister, but received only downcast looks and vague responses to the effect that she was to be found in the royal palace. When he enquired after his mother Eleanor, he was advised that she had taken refuge — along with several ladies, including a princess from Iberia — in the convent attached to the magnificent cathedral of Saint Mary of the Assumption.

More than a little confused by the people's wary response to the arrival of the English army, Richard's initial instinct was to suspect Philip and the French force of treachery. In an abundance of caution, he ordered everyone back outside the town's walls, and they set up their usual travelling camp. Three nights later, he was visited by a brother in the robes of the Order of St Benedict, who bowed obsequiously and offered to escort Richard and a small number of his men through a series of back lanes that led to the cathedral.

'Why should we creep there like foxes stalking a henhouse?' Hugh asked at Richard's elbow as the cathedral loomed into sight in the light of the half moon, and the chanting voices of both men and women could be heard in separate chapels.

'The monk said to keep our heads low and our voices still,' Richard whispered back, 'and if you value your head, do as we were told.'

A few minutes later, they were ordered to halt in the garden just before the nuns' cloisters, to allow some twenty or so robed and cowled figures to shuffle their way into the dormitory beyond. Their guide then beckoned them forward into the chapter house of the convent, where three women were seated by a low-burning open fire. Eleanor rose quickly as she saw them being furtively slid through the door, and hurried across the narrow room to be reunited with her son, while Adele threw her arms around Hugh's neck. The third woman sat silently staring at Richard until Eleanor gestured towards her.

'Behold your bride-to-be,' she said.

Richard looked across at Berengaria briefly. 'Very comely, I'm sure,' he commented, before anxiously looking back at Eleanor. 'Why the secrecy, Mother? Why is this town so silent and unwelcoming?'

Eleanor grimaced. 'We have been told to abide here and mind our own business. But at least we are free to move around. Your sister Joan is a prisoner of the man who has usurped her throne.'

'How can this be?' Richard demanded. 'She was loved by all, or so we were always assured in her letters.'

'She clearly was *not* loved by her husband's cousin Tancred,' Eleanor replied frostily. 'No sooner had King William died than Tancred seized the throne of Sicily and confined Joan to a suite of rooms within the royal palace. When we arrived and enquired after her, we were told that local matters were no affair of ours, and that we should go back to where we had come from. When I advised those sent by "King" Tancred that we had arranged to meet you here, he relented somewhat and allowed us to seek sanctuary in this abbey.'

'So he is apprehensive of my likely reaction to the imprisonment of my sister?'

Eleanor nodded. 'I gained that impression, certainly.'

'What has been his reaction to the arrival of the French under Philip?' Richard asked next. Eleanor shrugged, and Richard turned to Hugh. 'Go back to camp, and return with a dozen men, armed to the teeth. We shall pay this upstart a visit before he's even sat down to breakfast.'

The sight of fourteen heavily armed men at arms, led by a tall man with a face like thunder who claimed to be the King of England, was more than enough to persuade a sleepy gate guard at the royal palace that discretion was the better part of valour. Even the inner guard, although not outnumbered, thought it best to enquire first of Tancred whether or not he wished to receive a visitor so early in the day. Within the hour, Richard and his escort had been granted audience. Richard wasted no time in niceties.

'I am King Richard of England, and outside your badly maintained town walls I have some eight thousand fully armed men who have been without action for many weeks, and would welcome the opportunity to flatten your pathetic capital. *You*, I am advised, have been keeping my sister confined, in the mistaken belief that you are entitled to the crown of Sicily. I care not about the merit of that claim, but I wish my sister returned to me unharmed. Make that *now*!'

A bewildered-looking Joan appeared a few moments later with only one armed attendant, and when she caught sight of Richard she gave a cry of joy and rushed into his arms. 'My dearest brother — *thank you*! You were ever the bravest of my brothers, and my heart melts to think that you have come all this way to rescue me!'

'I haven't,' Richard replied brusquely as he pushed her gently aside. 'I am here on my way to wreak havoc among the heathens of the Holy Land, and only learned of your plight when I met up with our mother in that large convent near the north wall.'

'Mother is here also? Oh, what joy!' Joan shouted as tears rolled down her pale cheeks. 'I had thought to end my days here, in that awful set of chambers that was in truth a prison. I still grieve for the loss of my dear husband, and this peasant who calls himself my cousin has no doubt stolen my inheritance.'

'How much?' Richard asked with renewed interest.

'It must amount to many thousands of pounds in English coin, but it had not been fully calculated by the time that Tancred invaded.'

Richard smiled and turned back to the man in question. 'That will fit very nicely into my war chest, so perhaps you might wish to make arrangements to have it delivered to my camp within the next day or so.'

Tancred, who had thus far remained silent, shook his head. 'You can take your poxy sister away with you, for all I care. It will save me the cost of her maintenance. As for her inheritance, you are forgetting that *I* am the rightful heir, not her.'

'So you decline to hand over the sum to which she was entitled?'

'Clearly your grasp of the Italian tongue is not as firm as you believed. In French, I believe it should be worded "*aller vous baiser*".'

Richard's face set like mortar in hot sun as he spat back, in perfect Italian, 'You just made a very bad mistake — for you *and* your whorehouse of a town!'

He turned sharply on his heel and stormed out of the chamber after commanding his escort to follow. They left the palace on foot, Joan scuttling along in the middle of the group and supported on one arm by the gallant Hugh Repton. Richard enquired of a street trader that they passed, and was advised that King Philip might be found in the *citadella* fortress by the harbour, which he and his immediate entourage had taken over without resistance immediately after disembarking. They swiftly strode the half mile or so from the palace and found Philip at breakfast. He looked up in surprise as Richard appeared in the ground floor chamber of what had once been the office of the local *commissaire* until he had been invited to make himself invisible.

'Are your camp provisions grown so paltry that you have need to join me for breakfast?' Philip asked with a nervous chuckle when he saw the expression on Richard's face.

Richard was in no mood for jests. 'I intend to put this miserable hole to the sword and the firebrand, for reasons that we need not discuss. I therefore give you fair warning that it would be better for you and your men to join us in our camp to the north of the town wall. That way, you and they will not be mistaken for potential victims.'

'Do you not seek my assistance?' Philip asked with an amused grin.

Richard shook his head. 'You have no quarrel with the usurper who calls himself the king, surely?'

'Indeed not,' Philip replied as he carved more ham, 'but my men grow restless, having been held idle for so long. A little rape and pillage would serve to keep them in order, I believe.'

'Whatever you decide, have your men out of danger from mine by nightfall,' Richard told him as he turned sharply and strode back outside.

Their next port of call was the convent attached to the cathedral, where there was a joyful reunion between Eleanor and her daughter Joan. Richard then advised them that for their own safety they should all return with him to the English camp, where they would be suitably accommodated.

'We would surely be more comfortable here?' Eleanor protested.

'Not when my men enter the town under cover of darkness, bearing flaming torches. They will clearly foreswear to commit acts of brutality within a cathedral and convent, but I fear that Tancred will seek revenge by capturing you and recapturing Joan, so it would be best were you to withdraw with me. Since the comely young lady sitting in the corner there is destined to be the next Queen of England, we must ensure her safety in particular.'

'You are most gallant,' Berengaria said coyly, 'but may my lady also attend with me? My hair, it is so difficult, and she has already learned how I like it.' She indicated a small, dark-haired girl seated near the entrance. 'Her name is Edwina.'

'You must *all* leave or risk peril,' Richard insisted, then turned to Hugh. 'Hugh of Repton shall be the personal guard selected to accompany his mother Lady Adele, along with

Berengaria and her hairdresser. Mother and Joan shall travel with me. Now, let us leave while we may.'

It was mid-morning when they reached the English camp, and the sun burned through their thin clothing. Hugh gave orders for a new marquee to be pitched in order to house Richard and his immediate followers, allowing the ladies to move under the large canvas that had previously been the temporary residence of the king. As he escorted them formally under the opening flap, then turned to leave, he almost collided with the small, dark girl called Edwina. He stopped himself in time, but only by catching hold of her in a hug intended to make their collision less violent. She looked up at him with big, dark eyes and smiled. 'Being in the arms of a strong, fighting man is probably the best thing that has happened to me since I left England along with your mother.'

Hugh blushed and tried to stop his heart from racing as he took several deep breaths. 'I feel sorry for you, if that be the case. Your life must be very boring.'

'It has its moments,' Edwina replied with another broad smile, opening her lips slightly. 'Feel free to bump into me again whenever the mood takes you.'

Hugh nodded dumbly, not trusting himself to reply. Instead, he walked back outside and began organising the men into groups of six, as instructed by Richard.

By the following morning, Messina was a mere memory of its former grandeur. Hardly a building remained intact, and those that had been cheaply constructed from local wood had suffered the worst, and they were now lying in charred squares roughly outlining where they had once sat in two-storeyed splendour. More than one head of a household had perished on the end of an English sword while vainly trying to prevent the looting of their wealth, or the brutal violation of their female family members. Every narrow street had at least one stiffening corpse to remind Tancred of his folly in defying the King of England.

Only one thing blunted Richard's sense of triumph as he stood on a low hillside, looking over the remains of the town while the sun rose mockingly across the narrow strip of water that separated Sicily from mainland Italy. This was the fact that Philip had reacted angrily to the discovery that within the best appointed English marquee was a beautiful princess of Navarre who had no obvious reason to be there. He had demanded an explanation from Richard, who had simply replied, 'Ask me in the morning. Right at this moment, I have the destruction of a town to organise.' It was now morning, and Richard stood awaiting the inevitable.

He watched Philip dismount, with an escort of three men, at the foot of the mound on which he stood and walk steadily uphill towards him alone. For a moment he stood silently by Richard's side, surveying the night's work, then remarked, 'She is your intended bride, is she not?'

'To whom do you refer?' Richard asked disingenuously.

Philip spat on the ground. 'The woman in your mother's tent. The one with the angelic face and all that hair on her head. You brought her with you from your southern estates, did you not? And since your mother would hardly be sharing a canvas with a palace whore, I assume that she is intended as your bride. What have you done with my sister Alys?'

'It is not a matter of what I have done,' Richard replied, gritting his teeth. 'It is more a matter of what my father did with her. And I emphasise "with" her, not "to" her. Either way, it would now be an act of incest for me to lie with her, married or not. Given that I am embarked on a holy Crusade, that would clearly not be appropriate. She is safe and well, and can be returned to Paris within a matter of days once I give appropriate instruction. As for the lady in the tent, she is Princess Berengaria of Navarre, and my mother has chosen her to be the next Queen of England.'

It fell icily silent, apart from the sound of Philip's rasping breaths as he sought to control his temper.

'I choose not to fight alongside a man who requires his mother to choose his bride. As of today, my army and yours shall make their own deployments against the enemy. My fleet is in all ways prepared for departure, and you will see their distant sails heading east ere the sun sets. I have wasted too much time waiting for a Crusade companion who proved false. Farewell, Richard. Would that it had turned out more honourably for you.'

With that he strode down the hillside, leapt into the saddle and spurred his horse hard towards his camp. Richard breathed out in long, slow breaths. It could have been a lot worse, he concluded. Now to see if Tancred of Sicily had changed his tune.

Before nightfall, a messenger had arrived from the palace with proposed peace terms under which Richard would depart Sicily on promise of payment of twenty thousand ounces of gold in compensation for Joan's looted inheritance, and an offer of marriage between one of Tancred's daughters and Richard's declared heir, the infant Arthur of Brittany. Richard sent Hugh of Repton to the palace with his formal acceptance of those terms, subject only to the caveat that the English army would not depart until its fleet finally made it through the Pillars of Hercules and into the almost landlocked ocean that led eastwards to Outremer.

They waited until, late one afternoon in early April, the lookout on the harbour wall recognised the square rigging of the *Salisbury Maid* and gave a joyful shout. He leapt onto his horse's back and rode hard for the English camp with the breathless news that the fleet that had left England almost exactly a year ago — and had since put into every port from Bordeaux to Naples before its commander was advised that Richard might be found in Messina — had finally caught up with them.

There was no time for recriminations, since the departure for the Holy Land had been delayed for long enough. Richard hastily organised the order of sailing after hiring even more vessels to take the excess booty that his men had extorted from Messina. He also arranged for his intended bride, along with her attendant Lady Edwina, his mother Eleanor and his sister Joan, to accompany the next leg of his Crusade. They would go with them at least as far as the western shores of Outremer — perhaps to Tyre or even Acre, if Philip of France had got there ahead of them and laid siege to the port city that was crucial to the recapture of Jerusalem but had recently fallen into enemy hands.

Richard had no hesitation in placing these important ladies under the protection of his trusted commander Hugh of Repton. For one thing, he knew Hugh to be chivalrous with women, unlike some of his other immediate underlings, whose battle-hardened experiences tended to make them coarse in their language and manners. Secondly, he could be sure that Hugh would take the greatest care of the small group, if only because one of them was his mother, and he had recently seemed to be growing close to another of them.

The Welsh-born attendant to Berengaria, Edwina, was the daughter of Marcher Lord Sir Edmund Llewellyn, Earl of Flint, and Angharad Caddell, daughter of one of the pre-eminent knightly families that farmed lands leased from the earl. Both her parents were of Welsh descent, but Edwina had taken more after her mother, with her lack of height, her rounded figure, her raven-black hair and her deep brown eyes. Familiar only with the tall, flaxen-haired ladies of Anglo-Norman descent who tended to grace the English court, Hugh found himself drawn to Edwina. Her entrancing, sing-song manner of speech, her ample curves, her engaging smile, her occasional fit of the giggles and her dark beauty rendered him spellbound, and unfortunately so tongue-tied in her presence that she regarded him as a strong, silent type.

On the other side of this rapidly deepening mutual attraction, Edwina was experiencing bodily sensations that were entirely new to her as she approached her seventeenth birthday. She had of course met many strong warriors in her time, either on the vast family estates along the banks of the Dee estuary, or at court, and several had approached her father, the proud Earl Edmund, with a view to marriage. However, her father was one of those exceptional men who actually considered his daughter's happiness to be more important than the making of a favourable match. More than one disappointed suitor had been sent away when the sensitive but stubborn Edwina had recoiled from the prospect of a physical union with a bearded giant who smelt like his horse and behaved like one of his hunting dogs.

Hugh was different, she had rapidly come to realise. For one thing, he appeared to bathe occasionally, but more importantly he treated her with deference and seeming respect. Edwina was not to know that his customary silence in her presence was borne of an awkward shyness that overwhelmed him whenever he was in her company, and when she compared it with the ringing, loud commands that he gave to the sturdy men under him, she concluded that he came close to being the romantic troubadour of legend. She saw him as a fearless warrior who could nevertheless be soft and gentle in the presence of his lady. She set out to ensure that she became that lady; the giggles and coy looks intensified, the occasional hand on his arm became less than occasional, and she dressed to emphasise what her mother had bequeathed her.

When the English fleet was finally ready to cast off from Messina harbour, the ladies under the careful protection of Hugh of Repton had been allocated the *Santa Cecilia*, a large and well-appointed passenger vessel that had been plying the routes between Messina, the Italian mainland and the islands of Greece for several years under the watchful eye of its captain, Matteo Russo.

Richard was anxious to cross to Tyre without delay, both to support the French contingent under King Philip that had already gone ahead, and to ensure that they didn't steal all the glory, and so he insisted that the *Santa Cecilia* set sail after the main fleet. Russo advised that the sooner they all cast off the better, because a heavy westerly wind was building through the narrow entrance to the Mediterranean through the Pillars of Hercules, and they had been known to pile massive waves down the main sea lane to Outremer.

Undaunted by this advice from an experienced sea captain with extensive knowledge of the local waters, Richard ordered the fleet to depart in lines of four abreast. Several hours later, it was the turn of the *Santa Cecilia*, and long before they passed the Greek Islands on their port bow the westerly wind was blowing hard enough to enable the pursuing waves to lift the stern of their vessel so high that the bow was plunged into the next wave ahead. The helmsman could be clearly heard above the screaming of the wind, calling upon his favourite saints to preserve them from extinction in the boiling waves, while Captain Russo kept up a stream of loud oaths as he stood alongside him, helping to prevent the wheel from slipping from their grasp.

Hugh and the ladies had kept well below decks, but this somehow seemed to accentuate the violent pitching and yawing of the aft cabin that had been made available for their use. Both Berengaria and Joan were vomiting as daintily as they could onto the wooden planks beneath them, having thoughtfully pulled back the carpet first.

Hugh forced himself above decks, clinging to the stair rope as he opened the stern hatch doors, only to see them wrenched from his grasp and hurled by the gale down the main deck. All sail had been taken in, so that steerage was now only possible by means of the rudder that was controlled by the wheel. When Hugh finally battled his way up the steps to the wheel deck, Captain Russo leaned down and yelled in his ear.

'We will founder if we continue on our course. We must make landfall before we lose more steerage!'

'Where?' Hugh demanded. All he could see, either ahead over the swooping bows, or to port and starboard, was a relentless wall of angry spray.

'Somewhere ahead is the island of Cyprus,' Russo yelled back. 'There are harbours there, although its emperor is said to be a wicked man. But we have no choice. Go down below and warn the ladies that they may have to swim for their lives!'

Hugh battled his way back below decks with the ominous tidings. Eleanor chuckled grimly as she ordered Adele to assist her out of her gown, leaving her in only her under-shift. 'We will be weighed down by our gowns, should we need to swim,' she told the other ladies. 'Follow my lead and disrobe!'

Hugh gallantly opted to return above decks, where Captain Russo was yelling instructions to his helmsman, and helping him pull the wheel hard to port. Eventually, through the spray, a set of cliffs became dimly visible. Russo pushed the wheel back a few degrees to starboard, instructing his helmsman to hold that course.

The cliffs glided past their port beam, then the bow of the ship was pointed to what looked like a channel leading inland. 'That is Episkopi!' Russo yelled in Hugh's ear. 'If we can clear the headland, we may find safer passage in the lee of these cliffs!'

The vessel lurched and creaked closer to the cliffs, and appeared to be travelling side-on to the massive westerly that threatened to drive them on past Cyprus. But at the last moment both captain and helmsman combined their strength in heaving the wheel hard to port, and called for Hugh to add his weight to the joint effort. As he did so he felt the pressure caused by the swell that they were battling against suddenly cease, and all three men fell to the deck. The vessel seemed to give a mighty jerk to starboard, and was then pushed by wave after wave towards the entrance to a bay that had just opened up before their eyes.

'The wheel has broken!' Russo screamed. 'We have no steerage left, and the waves will take us where they will. *Dio ci preserve! Santa madre ci salvi!* Pray for your life, Englishman!'

IX

Hugh was vaguely aware of staggering back along the deck and yelling down into the stern cabin that the women should come up on deck and prepare to jump into the raging foam. Joan was first on deck, followed by Berengaria, both of whom clutched the bulwarks in an effort to steady themselves, then leapt overboard once they came level with the sea's surface.

Next out of the stern cabin was Eleanor, led by Adele. Both women were well into middle age, and in fact Eleanor was by now fairly described as 'elderly', but Hugh knew that his mother could swim, since she had taught him how. He therefore had no fear when she took Queen Eleanor by the hand and promised that she would ensure her safety if she would trust her for long enough to follow Joan and Berengaria overboard. Eleanor grimaced, white-faced, as she yelled back, 'If you should prove to be leading me to my death, my son shall hear of it!'

Hugh was mentally noting that the old lady clearly hadn't lost her mawkish sense of humour as he turned to Edwina, clad in the flimsiest of under-shifts, staggering towards him as she clutched the bulwarks. 'I can't swim!' she cried. 'Please, Hugh — I can't swim!' With that her legs buckled under her, and Hugh had just reached her side when the vessel seemed to jar against something under its keel, pitching sideways and throwing them both across the deck and into the churning surf.

Hugh's only thought was to keep firm hold of Edwina as they tumbled through towers of salty water. Then, after what seemed like an age, the sudden realisation that he had been flung down onto something soft but firm that alerted Hugh to the reality of their situation. He tentatively lowered his legs in order to confirm that they were in fact in only five feet of water. By lifting his feet as he felt the next swell coming, still with Edwina clinging to him and shrieking in fear, he could steer them both further onto solid ground. The ground in question was a stretch of sandy beach between two outcrops of rock. As Hugh pulled Edwina clear of the water, he was able to drag her further onto dry land.

Hugh lay for a few moments, thanking God for his survival and drawing in lungfuls of precious breath, before looking around him in hope. He saw Eleanor first, seated on a low rock that was covered in seaweed, with Adele by her side, holding her head down while she spewed seawater. A few yards away, in a shallow pool between two lower rocks, sat Berengaria, attempting to stem the bleeding from a deep gash on her left leg, and whimpering as salt water bit into the open wound. Finally there was Joan, on her knees in prayer and gazing across to where Hugh was staggering to his feet.

'Your companion would seem to have lost all her attire,' Joan yelled into the wind with a broad smile on her face.

Hugh looked behind him, to where Edwina had risen to her knees. 'Make the best of the view while it is still available, for you will not see me like this again unless we are married,' she shouted.

They gathered in a bedraggled group behind a large rock that rose out of the sand, providing some rudimentary cover against the driving westerly wind. It was, Hugh calculated, late afternoon, and what little sun was visible through the low cloud gave them no warmth. Once they had all regained their breath, it was Eleanor who stated the obvious.

'We cannot remain here, I suggest. Night will fall ere long, and we are soaking wet. The sea didn't get us, but an ague will if we don't acquire some more clothing, and a better shelter against this dreadful wind.'

Hugh looked up at the rugged foreshore, and could vaguely make out a hut of some sort a few hundred yards away, with smoke blowing sideways as it exited a hole in the roof. 'That looks like a fisherman's cottage or something,' he told the women. 'At least we could be out of this damned wind if we could prevail on someone to take us in.'

They half staggered, and were half blown, towards the squat building whose turf sod roof appeared to be on the point of being peeled off by the howling gale, and Hugh hammered on the door. A surly, middle-aged woman came to the door, and made some sort of enquiry of them in a language that none of them could comprehend. Hugh and Eleanor between them tried several languages, until the woman appeared to respond to Italian, and Hugh persevered.

He pointed back to where the superstructure of the *Santa Cecilia* was lodged further down the beach, her bow rammed into the sand. Deckhands were climbing off the wreckage into several feet of surf. 'Shipwreck!' he yelled in English, before correcting himself and offering, '*Naufragio!*'

The woman nodded sagely and beckoned them all into the single room, in which a driftwood fire was burning fitfully. In the far corner sat a gnarled, middle-aged man smoking a pipe. The women immediately rushed to the fire, where they stood dripping and shivering.

The woman gave the naked Edwina a disapproving stare, then moved to a box under the rudimentary table, from which she removed an old woollen cloak that she handed to her. The woman then extracted various peasant garments that the ladies shared gratefully among themselves.

She yelled an instruction to the man, who eased himself out of his corner chair with a resigned sigh and walked out into the still howling gale. She then removed a pot from above the fire, took a ladle from a hook near the door and emptied some sort of potage into a wooden bowl that she handed to Eleanor, who was visibly the most senior of her house guests. With grateful thanks, Eleanor put the bowl to her lips, then removed it quickly with a squeal of pain.

'It's very hot,' she complained, 'and it is most likely some sort of goat stew, to judge by the taste, but it will keep us alive until we are rescued.'

One by one the women took careful mouthfuls of the stew from the bowl, which was refilled twice before it got to Hugh, who confirmed with a mild curse that it was indeed goat. They had just begun to revive their spirits and dry out when the door to the hut opened and the man re-entered, followed by three men dressed as soldiers. Their apparent leader addressed them in Italian.

'You are from that ship that has foundered in the bay?' he asked.

Hugh nodded as he took it upon himself to answer for them all. 'This lady,' he told the soldier with a gesture towards Eleanor, 'is the Queen Dowager Eleanor of England, and her son, King Richard, is somewhere to the east of here, with a battle fleet on its way to recapture Jerusalem. The young woman to her right is Princess Berengaria of Navarre, who is betrothed to King Richard. The lady who is holding the bowl of stew is Joan, the former Queen of Sicily, and the remaining two ladies are attendants. I am Hugh of Repton, lieutenant to King Richard of England.'

'*Regale?*' the man asked.

Hugh nodded eagerly. '*Si — regale!* Royalty!'

The soldier then said something to the old man and woman, who nodded. The man held out his hand for the few coins offered to him by the soldier, who turned smartly on his heel and left the hut.

'What now?' Eleanor asked.

'I think that our hosts just received payment for our overnight accommodation,' said Hugh. 'As for what happens next, who knows?'

They spent the night huddled together around the fire, and Hugh was far from protesting as Edwina selected him for her sleeping companion. They awoke fitfully the following morning to another bowl of goat stew, and some liquor that tasted like nettles but had a kick to it. Hugh ventured to peer outside the hut, after the ladies had taken it in turns to make their ablutions in the nearby sand dunes. He discovered that the wind had subsided, and that the new day was cloudy but reassuringly warm.

They were listlessly debating what they should do next when the decision was taken out of their hands. They heard the rumble of wheels outside and a shouted command, followed by the wrenching open of the hut door. There stood a man in what looked like a somewhat overdone military uniform, dripping in braid and ribbons, but with a very efficient-looking sword swinging from a belt around his waist. He bowed sarcastically and introduced himself.

'I am Nikolas Ioannou, General in the Imperial Army of his Excellence Emperor Komnenos of Cyprus. You are to come with me.'

'We are to be guests of your emperor?' Eleanor asked graciously.

General Ioannou smiled back coldly. 'You are indeed, for as long as your ransom remains unpaid. Please accompany me to your wagon.'

X

William sat, stern-faced, as he listened to the events being described to him by the High Sheriff of Yorkshire, Osbert de Longchamp, brother of William's immediate superior William de Longchamp, England's Joint Justiciar. They were seated in the cramped parlour of the cottage in Bootham Bar, conveniently located near the north gate of the town, which was made available by the town officials to its senior constable, Edwin Mackenbury.

Constable Mackenbury had first told William of how he had been called to a wild disturbance outside the house formerly owned by the wealthiest Jewish man in York, who'd been named Benedict. He had been one of those killed in the riots that had followed the king's coronation in London the previous year.

Sheriff de Longchamp described the disgraceful events that had followed. 'The family had remained in the house since Benedict's death, but a local landholder called Richard Malebisse still owed money to the business that had been kept on by Benedict's widow, a woman called Rachel. Malebisse seems to have led the mob that surrounded the house and set fire to it, waiting for the family to run from it in panic, in order that they might be slaughtered. He was heard shouting loudly that Benedict had originally travelled to London to give money to King Richard that had been left for safekeeping by him from tithes and taxes imposed on various lands surrounding the town. Since he was one of those landholders, he was believed.'

'But it was not true?' William asked.

De Longchamp let fly a curse. 'Of *course* it wasn't true! But it suited Malebisse to spread that belief, since the Jewish community in York have long since been hated for their presumed wealth and seeming immunity from the normal taxation processes. And in any case, Malebisse was not alone. He was soon joined by two of his fellow landholders, Philip de Fauconberg and Marmaduke Darrell, who told similar lies. Finally, William Percy — who of course is a distant relative of the well-respected former Earls of Northumbria — added that he had been present when King Richard had given the command that all the Jews in England, to whom he owed money, should be done to death.'

'Similar rumours were rife in London at the time of the coronation,' William told him with a grimace, 'and this is said to have led to the slaughter there.'

'Well, it certainly had that effect here, but in a different way,' de Longchamp nodded. 'The family of Benedict managed to escape and take refuge in the old castle that you see on the river bank. Word spread among the Jewish community that a large mob was on the loose, intent upon burning down their houses and killing them. Before many minutes had elapsed, they had joined Rachel Benedict and her children in the castle keep, where they sought the protection of its royal constable. The constable left the keep for the purpose of ordering the rioters, in the king's name, to disperse, but when he returned he found that the Jews had become so fearful that they refused to allow him back in. This is when he called upon Edwin here to assist him.'

Edwin Mackenbury nodded and took back the narrative. 'I'd been with two of my colleagues, trying to hold back the growing mob and organise men to extinguish the burning buildings, before the fire could spread through the town. It was then that I was summoned to the castle, but I learned later, from Alwyn Dewsbury, one of my constables, that Malebisse organised a group of men to wait outside some of the houses that were about to be set on fire. Then he approached the houses and offered those inside safe passage out of the town if they would come out; when they did so, his fellows fell upon them and did them to death. I did not of course see any of this for myself, but Alwyn is willing to give testimony.'

'So you went to the castle,' William prompted him. 'What happened there?'

Edwin's face grew pale. 'By the time I got there, I could see smoke rising from inside the keep — which was constructed entirely from wood — and within minutes it was consumed by fire. We learned, from a small child who'd crept out of there before the flames took hold, that those inside — the Jews who'd taken sanctuary there — had chosen to take their own lives, at the urging of one of their religious leaders, rather than be captured or slain by hands that they regarded as heathen. All in all, that night we lost well over a hundred of our Jewish citizens, either by their own hands or at the hands of Malebisse and his evil companions.'

'And where are Malebisse and the others now?' William asked. 'Are they in secure custody?'

Sheriff de Longchamp shook his head sadly. 'I've been ordered to organise an inquest only, which will of course give the malefactors time to escape, if they haven't already. I was expressly ordered, by the justiciar, that there were to be no arrests. Local rumour has it that Malebisse and Percy are planning to join King Richard on Crusade.'

'Why would your brother seek to interfere with the course of justice in that way?' William asked. 'When last I spoke with him, he was most anxious to suppress any rumour that King Richard's was the hand behind the persecution of Jews in England.'

De Longchamp shook his head. 'I should have explained more clearly. There are two justiciars, are there not, with equal and joint authority? It was the other one — the High Sheriff of Northumbria — who told me that if I placed anyone on trial, I would lose my office.'

'De Puiset?' William asked, horrified. 'Did you not also make enquiry of your brother as to how to proceed?'

'I did, and he advised me that de Puiset had the support of Prince John, and that if I disobeyed his order I might be hanged, as well as losing my office. I have a wife and three children, my lord.'

'But it was Prince John who commanded me to come here and enquire as to what had transpired,' William explained. 'Why would he do that, after giving instruction that there is to be no trial for those murderers who deserve to hang?'

De Longchamp gave him an embarrassed and confused look. 'I was told that you had been commanded to conduct the inquest, and that I was to stand aside, my lord.'

William gave him a long, hard look. 'If you were to conduct that inquest, would you ensure that sufficient evidence emerged to entitle me to try Malebisse and his companions for murder?'

'For myself, yes,' de Longchamp confirmed, 'but I have to think about the possible fate of any of my constables who testifies against them at any such trial.'

'You fear that they would suffer reprisals?' William asked, sudden alarm written across his face.

De Longchamp and Mackenbury exchanged nervous glances, and de Longchamp finally spoke for them both. 'Last year, before Edwin became senior constable, the post was held by a man called Godwin Malleson. He was ordered to travel out to a place called Stockton, to arrest an outlaw calling himself Ned Skelton, although his real name was Edward Skillingham. He'd been outlawed for inflicting violence on a bailiff employed by his local lord when he sought to evict him and his family from their cottage for non-payment of rent. When Godwin rode into the woodland where Ned was said to have taken refuge, he was taken prisoner by several men who'd joined company with Ned. He was only released after he promised to approach the local lord with a view to cancelling the original debt, and seek my intervention in the matter of his assault on the bailiff.'

'And did he?' William asked, although he'd already anticipated the answer.

'He did indeed,' de Longchamp replied in a hoarse whisper, 'and when I passed on the matter for instruction from de Puiset, I was told to have Godwin arrested for sedition and confined within his own lockup. There was no trial as such, simply a further command from de Puiset, and Godwin was hanged in the Gallowgate three weeks later.'

It fell silent as William pondered the implications, then asked a few supplementary questions. 'Why was there no trial?'

De Longchamp shrugged. 'I was advised, in a dispatch from Justiciar de Puiset, that Godwin was guilty of sedition by the sole judgment of Prince John, exercising the prerogative power he had been handed by King Richard upon his departure on Crusade. That being the case, then he might be lawfully hanged, on pain of my being accused myself of dereliction of duty.'

William was horrified. 'So an honest man — an officer of the law — was hanged on the authority of Prince John, and nothing more?'

'That is correct, on the grounds that he had been guilty of sedition.'

'And what form had this alleged sedition taken?'

'"Assisting an outlaw", as I was advised.'

'And the man had been outlawed because he resisted the eviction of himself and his family from his landholding?'

'That was indeed the case,' de Longchamp confirmed. 'It was I who signed the eviction order, along with many others at that time.'

'Because those concerned were in arrears with their rent?'

'Yes, but so were many landholders in this part of the country. It was a bad harvest, followed by a harsh winter.'

'So it was on my estate,' William told him, 'but I sought no evictions.'

'Then your tenants must regard themselves as fortunate,' de Longchamp said. 'But you can perhaps understand why I am reluctant to disobey de Puiset's lawful command?'

'Whether it be lawful or not is a moot point,' William replied with a frown, 'but you must clearly proceed on my instruction, and step aside in order to allow me to hold the inquest myself.'

'And if the constables are fearful of giving the testimony that will justify the arrest of Malebisse and the others?'

'That will not be necessary,' William told him as his jaw set in defiance, 'since I am authorising their arrest *now*, on the basis of what I have learned this morning.'

'On your own head be it,' de Longchamp muttered.

William smiled grimly. 'That we shall see, my friend. That we shall see.'

XI

King Richard stood on the quayside at Tyre, gazing anxiously across the water for sight of the vessel that contained his mother, his sister and his bride-to-be. Behind him lay the heavily fortified city that had become the last stronghold of the Christian Crusaders following the capture of Jerusalem by Saladin three years previously. It contained several armies under the command of Western monarchs and potentates, who were now squabbling among themselves as to how best to retake the Holy City, and one of those — Guy de Lusignan — was standing by Richard's side.

Guy was nominally a vassal of Richard's for his estates in Poitou, but he had until recently enjoyed a more exalted status. He had been King of Jerusalem by dint of his marriage to Sibylla, the oldest daughter of its former king, Amalric, but in the Battle of Hattin he had been disgraced and humiliated by Saladin's forces, who had re-captured Jerusalem. He had been imprisoned for a while by Saladin, but then released, and was now nursing his ruptured pride behind the walls of Tyre, which was under the effective command of his de facto brother-in-law Conrad of Montferrat. Conrad was also claiming the title to Jerusalem by virtue of being the husband of Queen Sibylla's half-sister Isabella.

Guy saw his opportunity as he followed Richard's gaze out to sea, and asked, 'You fear that they may have foundered in that dreadful storm?'

Richard nodded grimly. 'Their vessel was not built for heavy ocean travel, and they were less than a day behind us. It has now been three days, and five vessels have failed to dock here in Tyre. The vessel bearing them is one of those, and I fear that they may have been shipwrecked.'

'The last ship to arrive here contained men who spoke of other ships foundering on the coast of Cyprus,' Guy told him. 'If their vessel was one of them, then they may have made it to shore, where they could have fallen into the hands of Emperor Isaac Komnenos. If so, then his reputation is such that you may expect to receive a ransom demand.'

'If he has laid a hand on any of them, I'll have his guts!' Richard yelled.

Guy placed a comforting hand on his arm. 'There is only one way to find out, is there not? I will gladly accompany you to Cyprus in order to learn the truth of the matter. I am your vassal for my estates in Poitou, and you may consider my offer of help as the payment of my knight service. It may also be that you can repay me with your support for my claim to Jerusalem.'

Richard laughed hollowly. 'We must *all* work in harmony if any of us is to be in a position to squabble over the title to the Holy City. But I will gratefully accept your offer, if you have men under your command familiar with Cyprus.'

Guy smiled reassuringly. 'There were many Greeks who enlisted in our Jerusalem garrison, wishing only to kill Turks. I have some left still loyal to me, and they may act as our interpreters.'

Five days later, a fleet of ten vessels moored in the harbour of Lemesos, known to the Greeks as Limassol. Richard sent one of his most experienced seconds in command to the emperor's palace with a demand for the release of any prisoners he might have who were from the English Crusade fleet. Emperor Isaac Komnenos sent back word that he had Richard's mother and sister, a young Spanish beauty, and two attendants, adding for good measure that they were accompanied by an impudent young man at arms who he would gladly return in several pieces.

Richard couldn't resist a chuckle. 'I think he means Hugh Repton. As for the prices he has placed on the heads of his captives, he may wish to pay that sum to me if he wishes to retain his throne.'

Richard gave the emperor twenty-four hours in which to hand over his prisoners unharmed, failing which his palace would be razed to the ground, with anyone seeking to defend it hung from its ruins. He also gallantly offered not to bind the emperor himself in irons.

The deadline expired, and the men at arms who had been brought across the ocean by Richard and Guy made short work of placing the entire island under their command. Richard and Guy then marched, side by side, into the palace yard with an army of a hundred heavily armed soldiers behind them, and accepted Emperor Isaac's formal surrender. He was then taken down into his own dungeons in order to personally unlock the door to the narrow room in which Hugh, Eleanor, Adele, Joan, Berengaria and Edwina had been confined for two weeks.

Eleanor and Joan rushed out and hugged Richard tightly, proclaiming their joy at being released. Richard recoiled from them both, then looked into the cell from which they had been released. 'That explains the smell,' he said as he wrinkled his nose in revulsion. 'Such conditions are fit only for beasts, so it is perhaps fitting that it will now be occupied by the pig who had you all locked up in there.' He turned to the three men immediately behind him, and nodded to Isaac Komnenos. 'Take him in there and chain him to the wall!'

'You promised not to bind me in irons!' Isaac protested through his interpreter.

Richard smiled sadistically. 'That is why I had these chains cast in silver. Enjoy your stay!'

The ladies indulged in the perfumed baths of the palace, now firmly under the control of Richard and his allies, and Hugh took to swimming in the harbour to reactivate his cramped limbs and reassure himself that he had not become afraid of water. Meanwhile, Richard set about arranging his marriage.

It took place on 12 May 1191, in a chapel he commandeered for the occasion, and was solemnised by Richard's own military chaplain, later to be rewarded for his services by appointment to the Bishopric of Le Mans. It was followed by days of endless feasting, courtesy of the commandeered palace kitchens, during the course of which Berengaria was crowned Queen of England by John Fitz Luke, Bishop of Évreux, for whom Eleanor had sent an escort of men and a hastily commissioned litter.

Once they had all regained their sobriety, Richard and Guy began making plans for the return to Tyre, and Hugh was summoned to their side.

'What think you of this local wine?' Richard asked of Hugh, hoping to establish a jovial atmosphere for what was to come.

Hugh smiled. 'A little thin for my tastes, sire.'

'You prefer the fruitier taste of Burgundy, perhaps?'

'Certainly, sire, but it remains a mere memory these days.'

'Not necessarily,' Richard grinned. 'You at least may enjoy its mellow flavour again ere long, and I would wish you to drink to my success across the water in Outremer.'

'Do you not mean *our* success?' Hugh asked nervously as he took in the implications.

Richard shook his head as he placed a friendly hand on his shoulder. 'No, Hugh, for I have a mission for you that is more important to me than the mere slaughtering of desert peasants. I wish you to journey back to Rouen on a most important Crusade of your own.'

'Sire?'

'Clearly, our mothers are fortunate to have survived their recent experiences, and are hardly best suited now to be journeying among the flies and diseases of the Holy Land. My mother has been there once before, as a young woman, and she has told harrowing tales of the conditions to be met once we leave the shores of Tyre and Acre. So she now stubbornly refuses to repeat the experience, and has specifically requested that you accompany her, and your *own* mother of course, back to Normandy, where she can learn of how matters fare in England in my absence.'

'I am flattered to be her escort of choice, sire, but there must be others more suitable than I to ride alongside two middle-aged ladies as they travel across France,' Hugh objected.

'I can only assume that you have not yet experienced the consequences of seeking to disagree with *any* choice made by my mother. But apart from that, I wish you to take the opportunity to cross the Channel in person and be reunited with your father, perhaps taking your mother with you. Thereafter, send me word of how my Chief Justice fares in his attempts to suppress crime in England. He was also charged with the duty of reporting back to me on any attempt by my brother John to stir up the nation in my absence. So far, there has been nothing, but that is perhaps because we have been so often on the move.'

'I had hoped to recoup my expenditure on all my new armour, not to mention my two coursers, by securing prisoners for ransom, or perhaps seizing rich goods in Outremer,' Hugh pouted. 'Then there is the matter of earning additional honour on the field of battle.'

Richard smiled indulgently. 'You have surely earned honour enough by saving the lives of two queens — one of whom was not then even crowned — from shipwreck on a Mediterranean island. That will not be forgotten, Hugh, and when we return to England you may anticipate receiving at least another earldom. As for your financial losses, I will of course ensure that you are more than adequately compensated out of my share of whatever spoils we bring back from Jerusalem.'

'The new queen and her attendant lady are not to accompany us?'

Richard shook his head. 'I require my new bride by my side wherever I go, since we are barely a week married. And of course she must have her lady in attendance, although I noticed that you and she were keeping close during the banquets of the past few days.'

Hugh and Edwina were happily becoming more and more intimate in their behaviour, and Hugh had been eagerly promising himself that it was only a matter of time before they lay together. Suddenly, the immediate future seemed less certain.

Richard sought to console him. 'She will no doubt still be waiting for you, and eager to renew your acquaintance, once the Crusade is over.'

'Depending upon its outcome,' Hugh reminded him glumly. 'And it is said to be unlucky to take a woman onto the battlefield.'

'Queen Berengaria will clearly not be going into battle,' Richard replied testily, 'and in fact she will probably be required to remain on the coast while we venture inland.'

'Would you not prefer me to remain by *her* side, to guard her in your absence, sire?' Hugh asked hopefully.

Richard's face set. 'You have your orders, Hugh, and I have already instructed six of the finest warriors from our force to accompany you all. You leave in two days' time.'

Edwina dissolved into tears when Hugh broke the news to her. They were sitting by one of the ornamental fountains that graced the central courtyard of the palace, constructed in an elegant oblong with porticos on all sides that resembled monastic cloisters. She appeared inconsolable as he placed an arm over her shoulder, and tried to reassure her that they would be together again once Jerusalem had been retaken. She looked up at him with tear-stained cheeks and attempted a pale smile.

'At least you won't be in the thick of battle, and from what you tell me neither my lady nor I will be anywhere other than Tyre, or perhaps Acre.'

'I will be gone from your side, but you will be ever in my thoughts,' Hugh assured her. 'When I reach England I will advise my father of our love, and I have little doubt that he will approve. After all, he also married a queen's lady.'

'But how do I know that you will not meet someone else, and make the same promise to her?' Edwina pouted.

Hugh leaned forward and kissed her on the lips. 'For one thing, there is no woman on earth who could inspire in me such desire as you do. And secondly, I am a man of my word, which I pledge to you now.'

The night before the planned departure, as Hugh lay sleepless, staring at the starry sky visible through the narrow window slot of his chamber and praying for a breeze, the door opened with a slight creak. A shadowy figure stood in the glow from the torches in the hallway.

'Are you awake?' came the voice Hugh sometimes heard even in his sleep.

He managed to reply that he was, although his throat grew dry. Edwina closed the door silently and moved towards his canvas bolster, unfastening her garment clasps as she did so. She halted, breathing heavily, by the side of his bed.

'You pledged your word already, so it is now only a matter of sealing the promise with your body, and in the eyes of God we are married. Are you prepared for that?'

'More than prepared,' Hugh whispered hoarsely as he held out his hand to assist her down onto the bed alongside him. 'Eager and willing would better describe it.'

XII

'Tell me exactly what you remember, and then tell me how much of it you're prepared to testify to in a court of law,' William demanded of Constable Alwyn Dewsbury, seated on the other side of the table in the high sheriff's chamber in York's Castlegate. Dewsbury frowned with a mixture of uncertainty and irritation.

'Just what I told the senior constable on the day, an' the sheriff a couple've days after that,' he replied. 'Didn't they tell yer?'

'Yes, they did, but I need to hear it directly from you. It's very important, and could lead to justice being done to the memories of all those who lost their lives.'

'Well,' Dewsbury reminisced as he put his head back, 'it were like this. That there Malebisse 'ad this mob wiv 'im, outside the 'ouse've that Jewish bloke what died in Lunnun. Malebisse were tellin' anyone that'd listen that the bloke went down ter Lunnun ter give King Richard all the money what'd bin collected in taxes an' suchlike from all the folk around York — even them what couldn't afford it. The two other blokes what was wiv 'im started tellin' folks as 'ow that were the truth, an' that the king wanted all the Jews in England dead, 'cos 'e owed them that much money.'

'There's absolutely no doubt in your mind about that?' William interrupted him. 'You're quite sure that according to Malebisse and these other two men — Philip de Fauconberg and Marmaduke Darrell — King Richard had given an order for the assassination of all the Jews in England?'

'Yeah, dead right,' Dewsbury confirmed. 'There were a third bloke there — that William Percy what owns 'alf've Yorkshire — an' 'e claimed ter 'ave bin there when 'e said it.'

'Perfect!' William muttered. 'But are you prepared to tell a court what you just told me?'

Dewsbury looked uncertain for a few moments, then sadly shook his head. 'The sheriff said as 'ow I could be took up fer "sedition" or summat if I did. That's what 'appened ter Godwin Malleson, an' 'e were only passin' on a message from an outlaw.'

William nodded sympathetically. 'I understand, but what are you prepared to say when I conduct the inquest?'

Dewsbury looked even more uncomfortable. 'Only that them what ran out've their 'ouses was killed by the angry mob, but I couldn't see who did what, it were that noisy an' confused.'

'Are the men you referred to — Malebisse, de Fauconberg, Darrell and Percy — still held in secure custody on my order?'

'All but Percy — seems 'e'd already gone off on that there Crusade, so 'e never got arrested.'

'But the other three were with him when he made that accusation against King Richard, and said nothing to disagree with it?'

'No, just the opposite — it were Malebisse what called on Percy ter tell the mob what 'e'd 'eard the king say.'

'Very well,' William replied grimly. 'Thank you for your courage in telling me what you saw. I can use that to considerable advantage in the forthcoming inquest.'

A week later, the upper floor of the guildhall was crammed beyond capacity. Constables were turning people away at the downstairs door when William took his seat behind the desk that was normally used by the guild alderman when he chaired the monthly meetings. The Sheriff's Bailiff was obliged to call for silence three times before the excited chatter fell to a level at which William could be heard.

'The next person to speak will be arrested for breaching the king's peace!' he yelled as he banged his staff of office on the flimsy desk.

There was still an annoying undertone of conversation among the hundred or so who were standing cheek by jowl on the dusty floorboards slightly below where William was seated as he called witness after witness. Apart from the two nervous constables who told of the angry mob outside the Benedict house, the fate that befell the remaining members of the family, and the deliberate fire-setting in the castle keep, the only other formal witness was the royal constable of the castle, Thomas Braintree, who recounted how he had been barred from re-entering the keep when he'd come back from attempting to deal with the mob outside the Benedict house.

It was then that William decided to become a little more adventurous. 'You attempted to disperse the mob who'd gathered at the Benedict house, but without success, is that the case?' he asked.

Braintree nodded. 'Yes, sir, and that's when I asked the sheriff to order his men to wade in and crack a few heads. I couldn't do much on my own, and my men were busy guarding the keep from another mob that was gathering.'

William smiled encouragingly. 'No-one has any cause to be critical of your actions, Constable Braintree. But do you recall any of the individuals who were part of this mob outside the Benedict house?'

'You mean their names?' Braintree asked uncertainly, with a look of alarm.

'Their names, if possible,' William confirmed. 'I should perhaps add that this is only an inquest into the deaths of those who perished that day, and the more witnesses I can hear from, the clearer will be my final finding. These people who you might be able to name will only be required as witnesses to what happened, and will not, I assure you, be charged with any misdeed.'

'Well,' Braintree replied with lingering reluctance, 'there was Nathan Pilger, along with Will Brinksley, who's married to Nathan's sister. But I never saw either of them do anything unlawful, and they walked away down Coney Street when I shouted that I was going to get the sheriff's constables to start making arrests.'

'And where might these men be located today?' William asked.

Braintree dropped his gaze uncomfortably, but there was a shout from those who had turned out to witness the inquest.

'I'm 'ere, an' so's Nathan!'

William invited each man to give an account of how they came to be outside the house of the Benedict family in the first place. They explained that they were on their way home after a game of skittles in The Three Tuns when they were drawn to the noise of a crowd in Coney Street, outside the largest house. Men were yelling for those inside to come out, and one man in particular was standing on an empty cart and telling the crowd that the man who'd lived inside it had been the one who'd taken all their hard-earned money, in the form of taxes, down to London, and that it was only fair that the house be burned down.

'Then,' Will Brinksley explained, 'this feller come forward an' said as 'ow 'e'd bin in Lunnun when 'e'd 'eard the king say as 'ow 'e wanted all the Jews in the country ter be killed, 'cos they was filthy livin' an' evil, an' wanted ter take our religion away from us.'

'Did you know this man?'

'O' course I did — everyone in York knows 'im, since most of 'em pays rent to 'im. It were Lord William Percy.'

'And the man you described who was standing on the back of the cart, urging the crowd to burn down the Benedict house — did he do anything to stop Lord Percy, or silence what he was saying about the king's order for all Jews to be slaughtered?'

'No — it were 'im what first said it, an' 'im what called Percy out from the crowd ter prove 'im right.'

'And did you happen to know who that man on the cart was?'

'Sure did. It were Dick Malebisse, one've the local magistrates in Acaster, what 'e inherited when 'e married the daughter've the previous lord there, another've the Percy lot.'

'So Richard Malebisse and William Percy are related by marriage, and both of them were trying to persuade the mob that King Richard had ordered the deaths of all the Jews in England?'

'Yeah, that's right.'

Thanking the men profusely for their honesty and courage in testifying, William made a formal finding that the Benedict family had died feloniously, at the hands of persons unknown, and that the Jews trapped inside the castle keep had died tragically, at their own hands. That concluded the inquest, and he thanked all those in attendance for their general good behaviour, before retiring to the back room for a mug of wine and some bread and cheese that Sheriff de Longchamp's wife had thoughtfully provided.

'That was the only appropriate verdict, I suppose,' de Longchamp conceded as he joined William in the back room, 'but does it take us any further?'

'You heard the evidence, presumably?' said William. 'Malebisse and Percy told the crowd that King Richard had ordered the murder of all the Jews in England.'

'So? How do we know that he didn't?'

'Because I was in his presence when he firmly denied even wishing the death of poor old Aaron Geller, who died during the London riot. But by spreading false rumours, Malebisse and Percy are clearly guilty of sedition, in the sense that it encouraged honest men to rise up against the supposed tyranny of a merciless king.'

'And what will you do about it?' de Longchamp asked.

William took a deep draught of wine, then swallowed the mouthful and laid down the empty mug. 'I shall draft attainders against Malebisse and Percy for sedition and send a copy to Justiciar de Puiset, to prove to him that the law in this portion of the realm will be administered as it was intended to be.'

William opted to remain in York, residing in the royal apartments at the castle, until there was a reaction from de Puiset. He did not have to wait long.

Less than a week after the issuing of the attainders, Constable Braintree interrupted William's breakfast for long enough to advise him that Justiciar de Puiset was awaiting him in the Constable's Chambers. William took his time completing his leisurely repast, then sauntered across the inner bailey with the air of a man who had not a care in the world, although his nerves were like bowstrings.

He was barely through the door of the Constable's Chambers before de Puiset turned sharply on his heel to confront him. 'I overrode those ill-considered attainders and freed the men you unjustly imprisoned. You are to report to Prince John immediately at the castle in Nottingham. In the meantime, you are stripped of your office. Is that clear?'

'What *is* very clear,' William grimaced, 'is that King Richard was guilty of very poor judgment in his eagerness to rescue Jerusalem. He will soon need to return in order to rescue England.'

XIII

'He had absolutely no authority for such an action!' de Longchamp protested when William presented his report to him in the Chancellor's Chambers in Westminster. A sixth sense had warned him to disobey John's command to attend upon him in Nottingham. 'De Puiset clearly regards himself as outside the law, but as Chancellor I can soon clip his wings. He should be suppressing lawlessness, and most particularly the current plague of outlaws robbing the unwary on our highways. You clearly seek to uphold the law in a tireless manner that does you great credit, but I suspect that Prince John is protecting de Puiset and his followers.'

'I fear that it has got beyond that,' William suggested as he accepted the mug of wine that de Longchamp poured him. 'Who would most benefit from the suggestion that King Richard ordered the deaths of all Jews in England?'

De Longchamp raised his eyebrows. 'You refer to John himself? With Richard out of the country, and clearly in no position to defend himself against such wild rumours, it would be too easy for John to assume power himself, which Richard feared he might do.'

'He said as much to me before his departure,' William told him. 'And you spoke a moment ago of outlaws. If the nation is seemingly overrun by them, then John would have a further excuse for taking overall control, claiming that he is doing so in order to preserve the nation from chaos and anarchy.'

'You suspect that he may be behind that as well?'

'I would not now reject such a notion. I had already heard of the existence of outlaw bands to the north of Nottingham before I rode to York, where there are similar problems. But these so-called "outlaws" are, in truth, bands of desperate men — and in some cases their families also — who have taken to living in the wild because they were evicted from their lands following the poor harvest and cruel winter that left them without the means to pay rent. The lords of their manors have clearly been encouraged to evict them, and fearful for the survival of their families the heads of household have resisted eviction, frequently with the use of violence. They have then been declared "outlaws" by local magistrates and sheriffs under John's control. This has given rise to the belief that the nation is now in thrall to wicked robbers, cutpurses and vagabonds.'

De Longchamp looked sadly down at the table between them. 'You paint a sad picture of a nation in chaos, William — perhaps precisely what John has sought to bring about. Queen Eleanor should be advised without delay, and urged to return. Do you have any tidings of King Richard?'

William shook his head. 'As you may recall, my son Hugh rides alongside him wherever he travels, but there has been no despatch from him since they were in Sicily, which was some months since. I am advised that Richard intends to put Princess Alys of France aside and marry the daughter of some monarch across the mountains south of Gascony, but other than that I know nothing more.'

'You say that John summoned you to Nottingham?' de Longchamp asked.

William nodded. 'However, I was not foolhardy enough to obey, and perhaps face being imprisoned, such is John's foul and wayward temper. He has inherited that much from his father, but unfortunately none of his grasp of kingship and what it entails. But it would seem that John has chosen Nottingham Castle as his base, certainly. Does it not remain under your suzerainty as Chancellor of England? I seem to recall that Richard was most insistent that the strategic line of castles built originally by William the Conqueror should remain under the control of the Regency Council.'

'The council has not met since the royal mother took her leave for Rouen, although I have of course been sending her regular reports. Most notably that her spiteful John has ignored many of the constraints that were placed upon him during the king's absence. For example, he recently seized the castles of Tickhill and Northampton in his own name, ejecting the seneschals that I installed, and threatening them with death for treason if they disobeyed.'

'Tickhill is little more than a day's ride north of Nottingham,' William pointed out. 'Could it be that John is seeking to establish a wide power base in the middle counties of the realm? If so, then I had best see to my own estate of Repton, unless he has already seized it in retaliation for my insolence in disobeying his command to return by way of Nottingham.'

'Have you courage enough to return there and enquire for yourself?'

'I most certainly have, not least because my younger son Robert is running the estate in my absence. He has a somewhat surly nature when crossed in any way, and if John has sought to seize Repton, then Robert may well be languishing already in the dungeons beneath Nottingham Castle.'

'Then lose no time in riding north,' de Longchamp urged him. 'If all is as it should be in Repton, then perhaps you might seek some opportunity to learn more about these outlaws of whom you spoke. If they have been reduced to that state merely through mismanagement of their lands by John and his acolytes, then I shall have further grounds for interference. In the meantime I will send word yet again to Rouen, alerting

Queen Eleanor of the pestilence that has descended on the land in her absence. Hopefully this time she will be well placed to respond.'

Queen Eleanor, in company with Joan, Adele and Hugh, was in fact in Évreux, as the guest of Countess Amicia de Montfort. Eleanor was much in need of somewhere to rest her weary bones for a week, or hopefully longer, at the end of a tiresome journey that had brought her small retinue, including several men at arms, overland from Marseille. They had gratefully disembarked there a month earlier, having found the Mediterranean much calmer than their last experience of it. They had then made the tedious journey north by horse, Eleanor having steadfastly refused the use of a litter, requiring Adele to also subject her ageing bones to a saddle. Once they had reached Bourges they had opted, rather than skirting too close to Paris, to avoid the de Montfort estate of Montfort-l'Amaury in the Île-de-France and had settled instead for the hospitality of the other de Montfort estate at Évreux.

This brought back happy memories for Adele, who had been married there to William in a ceremony that had also included two other nuptials. The young Earl of Chester, Hugh de Kevilioc, had married Bertrade, daughter of the *seigneur* of the Montfort estates who had also been the father of their current host, Simon de Montfort. In that same ceremony the younger Simon, who had recently inherited the estate of his dead father, had been betrothed to Amicia, daughter of the previous Earl of Leicester, Robert de Beaumont. She had at the time been a small child in the nursery, necessitating that the actual wedding be delayed a few years. Now, she was the mature Countess of Évreux with several children of her own, including yet another

Simon who, although still only fifteen years old, was eager to crusade against heresy, wherever it might be found.

'I worry incessantly about him,' Amicia complained to Adele as they sat in the shade of the manor house portico, watching the sun disappearing behind the range of wooded hills to the south west. 'You are fortunate that your own son has now reached a mature age at which all those gallant — and therefore dangerous — ambitions have been exchanged for more mature notions of marriage, fatherhood and a less hazardous life at court.'

Adele gave a dainty laugh. 'That may be so for many sons, but Hugh has yet to settle down in that manner. He would, even now, be risking his life alongside King Richard, had he not been ordered to act as guide and escort to the Queen Dowager Eleanor, and therefore myself. As for his taking a wife, I fear that my only grandchildren will come through my daughter Joan, at home on her English estate, and probably now nursing her firstborn, or my much younger son Robert, in charge of our Repton estate and no doubt rolling in the haybarn with a buxom country wench.'

'But you do not regret that marriage ceremony all those years ago, here at Évreux?' Amicia asked.

'Never for one day, although William and I have often been separated for many months at a time, as the result of our differing duties,' said Adele. 'You?'

Amicia sighed. 'I had one warrior for a husband, and I now have another for a son. My late husband, the previous *seigneur* of the de Montfort estates, died on his way to the Crusades, and only the need to escort his body safely home kept my warlike and deeply religious son from joining the latest attempt to retake Jerusalem. I had grown up, while a girl, dreaming of being the lady of the manor on some portion of the estates of the Earldom of Leicester, but here I am, on the borders between two powerful, and usually warring, nations.'

'At least for the present the two nations are united on Crusade against a common enemy,' Adele observed.

Amicia turned in her chair to look intently at Adele. 'Are the rumours true, that King Richard has cast Princess Alys aside and married a lady from Navarre?'

'True enough,' Adele told her. 'I was present at the ceremony.'

'Then England and France will once again be at each other's throats, will they not?' Amicia asked nervously. 'Then our homages will once again be split — to France for Montfort-l'Amaury, and to England for this estate here at Évreux, in the heart of the Vexin.'

'That will depend on many factors,' Adele insisted, 'not the least of which will be whether or not Philip of France can find another suitable husband for his sister. Let us worry about those things that are, rather than those things that may be.'

Almost immediately after the party had settled into their chambers, and while Adele was helping Eleanor to unpack, the entrance of Walter de Coutances, Archbishop of Rouen, was announced. He flustered in with a bundle of despatches under his arm.

'Forgive the intrusion, Your Majesty,' he began in his usual ingratiating manner, with a musical lilt familiar to those who had to tolerate his sermons from the pulpit, 'but there was much awaiting me on my return that I must bring to your attention. You will forgive my having broken the seals, but in the circumstances…'

'Yes, yes, just get on with it, Archbishop!' Eleanor interrupted him testily. 'I am anxious for my supper, but I suppose I must attend to matters of state prior to that.'

'That would be wise, with respect,' Coutances murmured as he handed over the bundle. 'I will, with your leave, take a seat while you read the despatches that have arrived here during your absence. They are from Chancellor de Longchamp.'

Eleanor began reading the despatches. She was soon sighing heavily, then the sighs became mutters, before the mutters became muted oaths. Finally she threw the last of the sheets down onto the carpet and looked disbelievingly at de Coutances. 'If I am to believe all that I have just read, then England is in chaos and long overdue my return.'

'Indeed, Your Majesty, that would also be my respectful advice,' de Coutances murmured as he shifted uncomfortably on his chair. 'I have no reason to disbelieve what your chancellor has written, although it is well known that de Longchamp and your son Prince John have long had their differences. But the garrisoning of royal castles is something that must be nipped in the bud, if we are to avoid another civil war.'

'You forget that Prince John is equally as royal as his brother Richard,' Eleanor reminded him.

De Coutances nodded, swallowed hard and replied, 'But he is not the King of England, and neither was he left by His Majesty with the authority to raise his own forces and take occupation of the likes of Nottingham, Tickhill and Northampton.'

Eleanor appeared to ignore that uncomfortable fact and moved on to other matters raised in the despatches. 'I am much concerned to learn that large areas of the nation are now overrun by outlaw bands that rob and murder at will. How can this have come about?'

'They are all landless and starving, Your Majesty,' de Coutances told her. 'The cause of that is said to be the insistence of their landlords that they forfeit their holdings for failure to pay the quarter day rents. Perfectly lawful, of course, but an impoverished and landless man will not shrink from robbery, and worse, when he sees his wife and children on the point of starvation. They have taken to our wide forest areas, it seems, and are feeding their families on royal game, which of course has provoked Prince John into seeking reprisals.'

'And these deaths of Jewish families,' Eleanor persevered, 'are they also from the same cause? Surely the Jews are not landed labourers, but wealthy merchants?'

'Indeed, Your Majesty, but it would seem from what de Longchamp writes that those deaths were at the hands of mobs misled into the belief that the Jews lay behind their current financial hardship. You will recall those dreadful scenes in London following the coronation?'

'I am hardly likely to forget them,' Eleanor replied with a faint shudder. 'And can it really be true that my son Richard is being blamed for these deaths?'

De Coutances bowed his head, as though fearful that Eleanor might land a blow on it when he replied as honestly as he could. 'So go the rumours, Your Majesty, although it is unlikely that anyone who knows him well would countenance such a suggestion.'

'That is what I fear, Walter,' Eleanor replied sadly, ignoring his clerical status and dignity. 'So few of his subjects know him other than what they see in public pageants such as his coronation. And it was doubly unfortunate that those Jews were killed on the very same day.'

'Doubly unfortunate without a doubt,' de Coutances agreed, 'but a golden opportunity for someone to spread wicked libels regarding who had ordered it.'

'And you are asking me to believe that it was Richard's own brother who was that "someone"?' Eleanor challenged him.

Walter bowed his head even lower. 'I can only pass on what de Longchamp reports to me, Your Majesty, although he claims that the same conclusion has been reached by the Chief Justice, the Earl of Repton. He was of course appointed by King Richard, so perhaps he might be accused of a certain degree of partiality where Richard is concerned. Mind, I have not had any reports direct from him — only what de Longchamp advises me.'

'And what of the other justiciar — de Puiset?'

'That is another issue you must give your mind to, Your Majesty. It would seem that the two justiciars are almost at daggers drawn. De Longchamp claims that de Puiset is in Prince John's pay, while de Puiset accuses de Longchamp of dereliction of duty, and the Chief Justice of bias in his persecution of those seeking to support John — two of whom he sought to attaint for sedition.'

'Have you any reports directly from Prince John?' Eleanor asked.

De Coutances nodded. 'Indeed I have, Your Majesty — he complains of attempts by de Longchamp and the Earl of Repton to undermine his authority. The difficulty there, as I perceive it, is that the true extent of Prince John's authority was never clearly defined. In the absence of King Richard, he must act to preserve the realm from lawlessness.'

'Lawlessness that de Longchamp and the Chief Justice attribute to John's manner of governing the country in accordance with constraints that were not clearly defined before we left?'

'You have summarised the difficulties perfectly, Your Majesty.'

'They are more than mere "difficulties", my lord Archbishop,' Eleanor replied archly. 'They threaten the stability of the entire nation. However, given the absence of King Richard on Crusade — and the need to maintain a royal presence here in Normandy against the threat of uprisings by local barons encouraged by Richard's absence — I do not feel that it would be appropriate for me to return to England at this time. At least, not until you advise me that I must step in and regain firm control in Richard's name.'

'I fear that such a day is not long distant, Your Majesty,' de Coutances murmured.

Eleanor nodded. 'Clearly, we need more immediate, direct and unbiased information regarding what is really going on across the Channel.'

'Indeed, Your Majesty.'

'Which is why I am instructing you to journey over there and discover the truth of matters for yourself, Archbishop.'

De Coutances paled slightly, but nodded his acquiescence nevertheless. 'Must I venture alone into what may well be a lion's den?' he asked meekly.

Eleanor shook her head. 'A man of God alone in such a place of turmoil would be as likely to survive as a chicken guarding a henhouse from a pack of foxes. You shall of course be accompanied by a retinue of men at arms. Yes, what *is* it, Adele?' she added in annoyance as Adele plucked at her sleeve.

'With respect, Your Majesty, might I suggest that my son Hugh be placed in charge of that body of men at arms? He has proved his valour in the field — or, perhaps more accurately, in the ocean — but his father, as you may recall, is the very Chief Justice to whom the archbishop referred earlier. Not only that, but our family estate in Repton is close to Nottingham, one of the castles that Prince John is said to have garrisoned with his own men. It may be that by sending him back in the company of Archbishop de Coutances — who is also the brother-in-law of my daughter Joan, married these several years to the Earl of Bodmin — we may acquire a truer account of how matters go in England.'

Eleanor pondered the suggestion briefly, then nodded. 'An excellent arrangement, and you may be the one to advise Hugh of my commission. If he remains in doubt, you may send him to me for a reinforcement of my command that he would be unlikely to forget.'

Back in Outremer, there appeared to be more animosity among the Crusade leaders than they were currently displaying towards the enemy. They had not yet progressed beyond Tyre, but open hostilities had resurfaced between Guy de Lusignan and Conrad of Montferrat regarding who was to be the rightful King of Jerusalem, should the Christian forces ever retake it.

Guy had previously occupied the throne by dint of his marriage to the heiress Princess Sibylla. But she had recently fallen victim to one of the many foul diseases that lurked in the hot, humid climate of the western shore of the Mediterranean, and her half-sister Isabella was claiming to inherit from her, at the urging of her husband Conrad of Montferrat. King Richard was obliged to support the claim of Guy de Lusignan, given the support he had received from him while rescuing his mother, sister and bride from Cyprus. However, the claim of Conrad of Montferrat was being championed by both Philip of France and King Leopold V of Austria, who had recently arrived in Outremer with a token force. They were related to Conrad as cousins in varying degrees, but it went beyond that.

Each had their reasons for wishing to remain on good terms with Conrad, given the location of his kingdom in Northern

Italy. Philip of France wished to retain good relations with the ruler who controlled the Alpine passes that bordered southern France, and the two monarchs looked askance at Richard's presumption in meddling in the title claims to a kingdom that he had thus far made no effort to retake.

Discord was simmering below the surface when the decision was made that it was time to move on Jerusalem, and that a good starting point would be to reinforce the siege of Acre, just two days' ride down the coast to the south, but closer to the Holy City. It had been threatened by Christian forces, with varying degrees of determination, ever since the fall of Jerusalem, but was consistently defended by wave after wave of enemy cavalry under the command of the mighty Saladin, behind whom all the Muslim forces had united.

Now it was judged that the time was right for a combined assault, given the recent reinforcement of the Christian army by the arrivals of the forces from England, France, Austria and elsewhere. In July 1191, leaving Berengaria behind the safe walls of Tyre, Richard took the initiative by moving on Acre with two monstrous mangonels that he immediately employed in hurling massive rocks at the crumbling and previously weakened walls of Acre. Although Saladin's forces were massed to the west of the city, and had previously been employed to good effect every time the Christians breached the walls, this time he ignored the pleas of its defenders to once again come to their assistance. The Muslim leaders behind the walls sent word that they were prepared to offer surrender terms, and on their second attempt Richard, in de facto command of the Christian forces, took the bait.

In the end he found himself negotiating with Saladin himself, although not face to face; in fact, the two leaders were destined never to lay eyes on each other. The negotiations stalled to the extent that although a prisoner exchange was agreed, the sum to be paid by Saladin for the ransom of his Acre garrison was never finalised. This did not, however, prevent the Christian forces from entering the city and engaging in the looting, raping and burning that were regarded as the perks of victory, but which did nothing for the image of their professed religion. Then it was time for the victory banners to be unfurled on the city walls.

Richard was watching the lions of England blowing in the stiff desert breeze, and muttered to himself when he noted the French fleur-de-lys banners fluttering alongside them, together with the flag of Jerusalem. Philip of France had taken himself home to deal with a succession crisis, but Conrad of Montferrat was obviously honouring his obligations to his ally in the matter of the crown of Jerusalem. Then Richard gave a yell of disbelief as he saw the red and white triband flag of Austria flying alongside his own. Leopold of Austria had supplied very few of the victorious troops that had taken Acre, and was already preparing to return home.

Taking a handful of his personal guard with him, Richard stormed onto the ramparts and tore the flagpole from its mountings. Then he and two others carried it down into the dry moat and trampled it into the dust.

Duke Leopold swore every oath within his repertoire when advised of Richard's actions. He finally hurled a wine mug through the entrance flap to his tent and yelled, 'One day, God help me, the arrogant bastard will pay dearly for that!'

XIV

It was Archbishop de Coutances' and Hugh's third day on the road from Dover to London, alongside their men at arms. Both the choice of port and the slowness of their progress were dictated by de Coutances' advancing years. Hugh was still cursing the duties that had brought him back to England, and even further away from Edwina, who for all he knew had perished somewhere in the desert sands of Outremer. He'd volunteered to organise the allocations of the men at arms leaving for Tyre, thereby delaying his departure for two more blissful nights with the woman he already thought of as his wife. This last memory at least gave him something to say to de Coutances in order to lighten the boredom for them both as their horses picked their way through the meadow tracks. The long slope ahead of them would, when breasted, finally give them their first view of the Thames, with Westminster on its north bank.

'Do you believe that a marriage between a man and a woman requires the blessing of a priest before God may be said to have given His approval?' Hugh asked.

De Coutances allowed himself a wry smile. 'I have seen many happy unions that were never celebrated in a church, and an equal number of marriages presided over by a member of my calling that were portals to Hell here on earth. Presumably you have the usual reason for asking?'

'That being?'

'You have promised marriage to a woman that you have lain with, and now seek some excuse to renege on that promise.'

'The first part only — I lay with a beautiful lady who I would wish to wed, and we pledged our troth before doing the deed.'

'And neither of you wishes to resile from that promise? If that be the case, then count your blessings and seek out a priest. What is your difficulty?'

Hugh sighed. 'She is high-born, and serves a queen.'

'And you serve a king, while your mother also serves a queen. You would be marrying into your own class, surely?'

'On one side, certainly. But my father is the Chief Justice of England, and may expect better from me.'

'He is only the Chief Justice because he was appointed by King Richard. Before that he was, effectively, a nobody. You at least enjoy the king's current favour, whereas your father's position may prove to be an uncertain one.'

It fell silent for only a moment, because Hugh had an urgent need to know the precise reason why he, and the dozen men at arms dawdling behind them, had been sent back from Rouen to guard its archbishop.

'You have been sent on a mission by Queen Eleanor, but not even my own mother would confide in me what that mission was. Are you here to oust my father from office, and if so, why?'

'My mission is to investigate the truth of certain information we have received from Justiciar de Longchamp. He is unpopular at court because of his refusal to speak English, his haughty manner with those beneath him, and his opposition to almost every action by Prince John. But he urges us to curb John's recent actions in response to a certain lawlessness that has blighted the realm — lawlessness that he claims John himself has fomented, in order to justify having garrisoned certain royal castles with his own loyal men. There is, of course, the rival argument that John has done so in the best interests of the nation, given the lengthy absence of its king on a Crusade that many people regard as being none of England's business. So you see, the issues are thorny.'

'Has any of this a bearing on how my father is conducting himself as Chief Justice?' Hugh asked nervously.

As usual, de Coutances was circumspect. 'There have certainly been complaints from Prince John regarding your father's seemingly relentless pursuit of certain nobles who, according to him, were behind the deaths of some Jews in York, although many of those deaths seem to have been by their *own* hands. However, it was your father's contention, voiced to de Longchamp, that Prince John was the real author of the unrest. Given de Longchamp's antipathy to Prince John, he obviously speaks of your father's actions, and seeming courage, with great praise. But the opinion I have from Prince John is that your father has become a mere tool — a mouthpiece — for de Longchamp.'

'My father is no man's lacky!' Hugh protested hotly.

'There speaks a loyal son. But unless my memory plays me false, when we finally breast this long hill we shall once again be in sight of the spires of Westminster.'

William rose quickly from behind his desk as he saw the two men enter his office chamber without introduction. He moved round it and hugged Hugh. 'God be praised — how fare matters in the Holy Land?' he cried. Then he realised that the second man was de Coutances and stepped backwards with a fearful look, examining Hugh's face for any sign of bad tidings. 'Why is the archbishop with you? What has happened in Rouen? Is your mother safe — and of course Queen Eleanor? We recently heard a rumour that they had been shipwrecked — do you come with ill tidings?'

'No, Father,' Hugh said reassuringly. 'There *was* a shipwreck, and I was also in it, but we all escaped. Mother is safely back in Rouen, along with her mistress, and the last we heard King Richard had reached the shores of Outremer, and was planning to march on Jerusalem.'

'Then why…?' William asked with a hard stare at de Coutances, who took the seat in front of William's desk and explained the purpose of his visit.

'We are constantly receiving word in Rouen that affairs in England are not as they should be. To be precise, we've heard that Prince John and Justiciar de Longchamp are at war, while the affairs of the nation are in chaos. Likewise, John writes to his mother that you are acting like a tyrant in the execution of your duties, and enforcing what you take to be the law in a manner way beyond the authority that was left to you by King Richard. I am here to learn the truth of how matters lie, and report back to the queen.'

'You presumably mean the *dowager* queen, and not the one that Richard is rumoured to have taken as his wife?' William asked. 'It bodes ill for England that he has rejected Alys so publicly, humiliating both her and France.'

'You need have no fear of reprisals for as long as King Philip is fighting alongside King Richard,' Hugh told him. 'Of far greater concern, surely, is the unrest *within* the realm caused by your war with Prince John.'

'It is not *my* war,' William replied as he slid back into the chair behind his desk, indicating for Hugh to take the remaining seat in the corner of the chamber. 'I answer to de Longchamp, and to him I report what I have discovered. The accounts he has no doubt sent to Rouen are based on what I told him.'

'And now you can report to me in person,' de Coutances told him with a smile, 'since I am commissioned by Queen Eleanor to put right any wrongdoings that may be threatening the tranquillity of the nation. Is it true, as Prince John maintains, that you attempted to pass an act of attainder on two men who were accused of being behind the murder of Jews in York?'

'Perfectly true,' William admitted, 'and perfectly justified. I had witnesses who could have testified that when the house of a prominent Jewish merchant from York was being fired, those two men — Malebisse and Percy — were claiming that King Richard had authorised the slaughter of all English Jews. That was not only a lie, as de Longchamp can attest, but it constituted the crime of "sedition". Such a heinous crime is deserving of attainder, and had the additional advantage that no trial would be necessary. This was important to the process of enforcing justice against Malebisse and Percy, because the witnesses in question were terrified of incurring the same reprisals that had been visited on a local constable who had sought to enforce the law against one of John's lapdogs.'

De Coutances shook his head with a mixture of sadness and rebuke. 'Surely, as Chief Justice and a man of legal learning, you should have well been aware that an act of attainder can only be passed by the Council of State — the very *Curia Regis* that you helped to establish during the reign of the previous King Henry. Little wonder that Prince John felt obliged to countermand your order, free those two men, and send a report of your abuse of office to Queen Eleanor — hence my presence here today.'

William reddened. 'You have no idea how pernicious has become John's stranglehold over the running of our justice system! He has evicted those unable to pay their quarter rents because of poor harvests and has given the land to those prepared to do his bidding. Then, when those dispossessed of their land are obliged to take to the forests and hunt the royal game to feed their families, he claims to be the peoples' saviour and protector against those he declares to be "outlaws". There are many in England who, although normally sensible and fair-minded, now believe that King Richard is a feckless adventurer who has left the nation in ruin, after emptying the Treasury and borrowing from Jews whose deaths he has commissioned in order to cancel his debts. John then sets himself up as the true friend of all Englishmen, and the only one of the brothers fit to rule the nation.'

'Those are serious allegations, little short of treasonous,' de Coutances murmured uneasily. 'And you have not yet made mention of the position being taken by de Puiset, the other justiciar.'

William snorted derisively. 'He is John's man, and seeks to clamp down on those now condemned as "outlaws". It may owe much to the fact that King Richard, before his departure, installed his own illegitimate brother Geoffrey as Archbishop of York. The see had remained vacant since your departure from it, and de Puiset therefore had no spiritual constraints on his temporal influence in that region. He lost much by Richard's actions, and was easily prevailed upon by John to assist in undermining the royal authority by way of revenge.'

De Coutances sighed again. 'On the one hand, I should be taking strong action regarding your overzealous abuse of power, which I am prepared at this stage to consider as simply an excess of outrage at what you discovered when you made enquiry. On the other hand, Queen Eleanor has appointed me as Chief Justiciar, to act as a mediator between the two existing justiciars. Not before time, from what I have learned this morning. But that raises another delicate issue, namely the risk of confusion arising between the roles and responsibilities of Chief Justiciar and Chief Justice. You see the problem?'

William's face took on a resigned expression. 'I am being stripped of my office?'

'Not entirely,' de Coutances told him consolingly. 'I propose that you cease being the *Chief* Justice, but take up duties as one of the Royal Justices. There is, I'm afraid, a shortage of them since Richard's departure, due to John's failure to replace those who have become too old and infirm to continue travelling the nation. But in your new capacity I wish you to bring me proof of those malefactions of which you accuse Prince John. I may then refer them back to Queen Eleanor with a view to having John's wings clipped if, as you allege, he is seeking to undermine the authority of King Richard during his absence.'

William nodded. 'I may begin in my own home paddocks, may I not? There is talk of an outlaw band in the Royal Forest north of Nottingham known as the "Shire Wood", where Prince John maintains a hunting lodge. My other son Robert has connections with a family living in the countryside adjacent to that, so I may make enquiry of them, and perhaps speak in person to those who have been driven off their land.'

'Thereby risking an accusation by Prince John that you are consorting with outlaws,' Hugh chimed in from the corner of the room, having maintained a discreet silence up until then.

'That is a risk I must take,' his father replied, 'as must you, since it is high time that you met your younger brother. And if I am to stick my head into an outlaws' nest, I shall need an armed escort, I imagine.'

'I had thought to journey west to Bodmin to meet my niece Rosalind,' Hugh pouted. 'She must be almost a year old now, and I have of course never seen her.'

'She is the most beautiful and angelic of creatures, apparently,' de Coutances replied. 'Or at least, so my brother advises me. You are not the only one to lay claim to being her uncle, remember.'

Hugh went slightly red in the face as he apologised for the oversight. 'It is all too easy to forget that my sister Joan married into your family, given your favoured position at Queen Eleanor's court.'

'I *have* seen the lovely Rosalind,' William told them both, 'and I bow to no-one in my superior claim as her grandfather. But you must travel north with me, Hugh, to protect your old father from the wrath of Prince John and his lapdog Sheriff William de Wendenal.'

On the fifth day of their journey, when they were little more than an hour's ride from the Repton estate, Hugh finally raised the issue he was anxious to resolve.

'Mother was a queen's lady when you first met her, was she not?'

'Indeed she was,' William confirmed. 'She served Queen Eleanor even in those days, despite being a sister of the Earl of Chester.'

'And your family had no objection to your marrying beneath you?'

William slowed the pace, forcing the four men at arms riding behind them to do likewise. He turned in the saddle to face Hugh with a stern stare. 'Two things, Hugh. First of all, I did *not* marry "beneath me", as you put it. I just mentioned that your mother came from the Chester earldom, so she was high-born, as many queen's ladies are. Secondly — and do not lose sight of this important fact — I was a nobody before I was fortunate enough to enter the service of the former King

Henry because of my legal training. My brother and I were raised as orphans, although we *did* have parents.'

'So I have an uncle who I have never met?'

'You *had* an uncle, once. His name was Alain, and he entered the Church for long enough to be killed defending Archbishop Becket against the knightly scum who murdered him. He and I were twins, and in keeping with the family tradition that I chose to uphold, our mother was in service to King Henry's queen, Adeliza. Her name was Elinor, and my father was a knight errant from Poitou, with family links to the de Montfort estate at Évreux. By a strange quirk of fate, that was where your mother and I were married, although both my parents had died by then. In fact, I never met them, my only family connection being with an uncle who periodically visited us in the monastery school in Norfolk and oversaw our welfare. So do not ever again even *hint* that I married beneath myself.'

'But what of me?' Hugh asked. 'Were I to marry a queen's lady, would you approve?'

William sighed with irritation. 'You have learned nothing from what I just disclosed, have you? For one thing, as I was at pains to point out, should you marry a queen's lady, you would be the third in line to do so. More to the point, my consent, and the blessing of your mother, would depend entirely upon the character and disposition of the lady in question, rather than her status at court. But fortunately for you, Lady Edwina is the daughter of an earl, and your mother approves of her. She could hardly do anything else, given that she herself recommended her as a lady to attend upon the new Queen Berengaria.'

There was a stunned silence before Hugh asked in a small voice, 'You already knew?'

'Indeed I did. In addition to bearing instructions from Queen Eleanor, de Coutances brought me a letter from your mother, singing her praises for your bravery, gallantry and fine manners, and advising me that you seemed in danger of losing your heart to a beautiful Welsh girl.'

'You should know that I've lost more than that to her,' Hugh admitted sheepishly, 'and we are pledged to each other. Subject to your approval, that is.'

'If she's good enough for your mother, than I will hardly be allowed to disapprove,' William chuckled as he quickened the pace. 'Now, let us see how many of those good manners you can display when you meet your long-lost brother. He may well come across as a bluntly spoken peasant, but do not be deceived. And he — or rather the sister he once thought he had, but who now would seem to hold his heart — may be the key to our discharging our mission to learn the true nature of Prince John's actions. There's the tower of St Wystan's Church up ahead, and I for one am ready for my dinner.'

Richard had finally lost patience with Saladin, and his delay in fixing a price for the ransom of what was left of his Acre garrison. There were almost three thousand hostages, herded into a compound in the centre of the city they had once guarded. Even though they were being kept at virtual starvation level, they were costing the Crusade army much in the way of provisions. The time had come, Richard decided, to force Saladin's hand.

He ordered that the prisoners be escorted out into the blazing hot desert, each of them tied at the wrists to the man next to him on either side. Their feet were left unbound, in order that they might shuffle over the scorching sand, those without adequate footwear screaming in pain. Two hours after they had left Acre, a few had collapsed with heat exhaustion, to be finally dispatched where they lay and unhitched from the column. The remainder were drawn up in lines resembling a besieging army, several hundred yards from the desert camp established by Saladin.

Richard sent word by messenger that unless the great Mohammedan general finally named the price he was prepared to pay in order to preserve his own fallen men, then they would be slaughtered before his very eyes. Saladin's only reply was to remind Richard that there were also Crusade prisoners inside the Bedouin camp. Richard's leading generals, along with those left behind to preserve their nations' honour for those monarchs who had already departed, pleaded with Richard to at least trade 'one for one' in order to preserve the lives of their captured comrades. However, the king was in no mood to display what he regarded as weakness.

Wailing pitifully, the Acre prisoners — all two thousand seven hundred of them — were ordered to kneel, and every man at arms who had accompanied them was ordered to draw his sword. The next command saw several hundred Crusader sword blades flash in the noonday sun as heads dropped onto the desert floor, each in its own garland of gore that rapidly soaked into the sand.

An hour later, a solemn procession was led out from the Arab tent enclosure. Several hundred Crusader warriors, of six different nationalities, underwent the same fate. The desert resembled a nightmare graveyard whose contents had been dug up by wild dogs, and King Richard had become as feared by his own men as he was hated by the enemy.

XV

Hugh gazed in fascination at the brother he'd known about for seventeen years, but who he was meeting for the first time. Robert was dressed in farm labourer's clothes and had an unruly mop of shaggy dark-brown hair. Apart from the height and the general facial similarity, it was difficult for Hugh to believe that they had come from the same parents, although he recognised something of himself in the youth's proud, and somewhat resentful, insistence to their father that the estate was running well, that there had still been no evictions, and that the upcoming harvest would be up to expectations.

'I'm not here to check on the harvest,' William explained patiently. 'There's something else I need your assistance with.'

'What's that?' Robert asked bluntly as he cut himself more of the cheese and manchet loaf in the middle of the table.

William lowered his voice slightly. 'This family that for many years you believed yourself to be a member of — they have relatives somewhere in the Shire Wood, do they not?'

'Yes, so what?' Robert asked. 'Thomas's brother has a farm holding in Edwinstowe, and the cousins all used to be regular playmates during visits. That was before Thomas declared that it was no longer safe to go visiting, although from time to time they still come to us, and Beth and her cousin Alice are still close.'

'I heard from you on a previous visit here that in the Shire Wood there are some families living rough, who were thrown off their holdings when they couldn't pay the quarter rents. I need to speak with them in order to learn how they were treated by Sheriff de Wendenal.'

'Beth could tell you that without the need to speak to them,' Robert assured him. 'Do you want me to go and get her?'

William agreed, and within minutes Robert was back, leading by the hand one of the healthiest looking women Hugh had ever laid eyes on. She was approximately the same age as Robert, but resembled a fully mature woman who'd lived all her life on the land. She was tall, with a full figure that was almost bursting out of what was no doubt last year's smock, and had long, light auburn hair bleached by the sun. Her hazel eyes glowed out from a sun-browned face, and if ever it were necessary to convince pasty-faced courtiers that life on the land was more beneficial for one's health and natural beauty, then Beth would be the one he would present for inspection, Hugh decided.

It rapidly became obvious that Robert shared his older brother's appreciation of Beth's natural attractiveness, since he did not let go of the girl's hand once during the conversation that followed.

'I'm sure as 'ow Alice an' 'er man 'Arold could tell yer what yer wants ter know,' Beth was reassuring William. 'They was lucky ter be workin' the land wiv our aunt and uncle, so they was able ter keep their cottage. But 'Arold's neighbour Ned Willows were thrown out by the sheriff's men, an' kicked round the 'ead fer 'is troubles when 'e tried ter resist. They reckon 'e's not bin quite right in the 'ead since.'

'Is he among the so-called outlaws living in the Shire Wood?' William asked eagerly.

Beth shrugged. 'Mebbe Alice could tell yer, but it's bin a while since we was up there, an' they say it's not safe in there fer ordinary folk no more.'

William sat thinking for a moment, then came to a decision. 'What I really need is to be able to meet with these outlaws, and find out from them how they came to be defying the authorities. I won't be acting in my capacity as a justice or anything — just someone sent by King Richard.'

''As yer really bin sent by the king?' Beth asked, clearly impressed.

William nodded. 'By a man sent by the king, anyway. But Hugh here serves the king directly, as one of his most trusted men at arms, while his mother — the lady of this manor — is still in service to old Queen Eleanor. Anything we learn about the hardships being endured by those families in the Shire Wood will be reported to King Richard when and if Hugh rejoins him on Crusade.'

The mention of the Crusade reminded Hugh that he was almost certainly more usefully employed fighting the enemy alongside his royal master — and, more to the point, protecting Edwina and her mistress Queen Berengaria as they sat by the ocean shore, awaiting the outcome of raids on Jerusalem. All this concern for landless peasants seemed to him to be misplaced. He had no remaining interest in either this modest estate on the banks of the Trent or the brother with the buxom wench who was no doubt already his mistress. But for the time being he'd remain, if only to protect his father from himself.

The likelihood that he would need to do so became more real and immediate when, in response to an invitation conveyed in person by Robert and Beth, the farm wagon returned five days later containing two more people. The introductions were hastily made on the manor house doorstep. Thomas and Meg Derby hugged their niece Alice, and her husband Harold, and invited them to meet their lord of the manor and his older son. The new arrivals then sat down to talk with William. They did so hesitantly at first, because on the journey from Edwinstowe Beth had regaled them with tales of how grand their master was, and how he came on a mission from the king himself.

'I need to know how those folk living in the Shire Wood came to be outlaws, and if they really do rob everyone who ventures along the North Road through it,' William explained. 'This is important for the future of the nation, believe it or not, because if, as it is rumoured by some, Prince John lies behind it all, we can get word through to Queen Eleanor that she should return to England without delay. She can then curb his actions and preserve the realm for the return of King Richard.'

'It's not really Prince John yer needs ter 'old ter account,' Harold Greenwood replied testily. 'It's that rotten Sheriff de Wendenal — 'e's the one what throws the people off the land, like 'e did Ned Willows, an' 'e's the one what's bin doin' all them killin's.'

'Killings?' William asked eagerly. 'Who has he been killing?'

'Anyone what 'e catches livin' off the land inside that there "Royal Forest", as they calls it. 'Cept it ain't the king's deer, is it? The deer were put there be God, an' if folks is starvin' then God won't mind if they snare one or two from time ter time, just ter keep the wolf from their door. But them what gets caught by the sheriff gets 'ung off the nearest tree, right there in front've their families. Then there's the ones what gets hauled onter the nearest village green an' roasted over an open fire what the 'ole village's ordered out ter watch. I only saw it the once, an' God 'elp me, I never wants ter see it agin.'

'That's utterly unlawful, and those responsible can be brought to justice and hanged themselves!' William retorted.

Harold turned and spat into the rushes. 'It's the *sheriff* yer talkin' about, remember? 'E does what 'e likes. When it 'appened fust, an' the village bailiff went ter the castle ter protest, 'e were locked in the caves underneath fer a month wivout food, drink nor even daylight. They sent 'is body back strapped ter the underneath've a bullock. We got our own back in a sense, mind you, 'cos we slaughtered the bullock an' 'ad a village roast.'

'That's utterly appalling!' William responded.

Hugh shook his head in disbelief. 'I've seen some pretty disgusting and inhuman things on the field of battle, but at least there's some excuse then. To do that to someone who was simply trying to report an injustice to the very man appointed to uphold it is a wicked crime before God!'

'God has little to do with it, I'm afraid,' William told them sourly. 'Sheriff de Wendenal parted with Christian values the day that he threw in his lot with Prince John. If we can get witnesses to what you've just described, Harold — people who are prepared to stand up in court and report what they saw and experienced — then the sheriff himself can be hanged from his own gallows!'

'Fat chance!' Harold replied. 'Them's all scared've what'll 'appen ter them if they says owt agin the sheriff an' 'is bully boys.'

'Not once we've restored law and order to this part of the country,' William insisted. 'The first thing I need is to be able to speak to these people, to assure them that it will be safe to come forward and testify.'

'Well, them's all 'idin' in the Shire Wood, ain't they?' Harold objected. 'Them's scared ter come outta there, an' yer can understand why.'

'Then I shall have to go in there myself and speak to them,' William suggested.

'Yer wouldn't last a minute in there,' said Harold. 'Them's all got bows, an' a few swords what they stole off folks they robbed. By all accounts, they doesn't respect noble folk like yerself anymore. In fact, if yer look like nobility, yer likely ter die even quicker.'

'He's got a point, Father,' Hugh added in rising alarm. 'At least let me accompany you with my small detachment of men at arms.'

William shook his head. 'As Harold already told us, these people do not respect rank, and thanks to Sheriff de Wendenal they have a justified fear of those in authority. As you know better than I, fear causes a man to act with sudden and ill-considered violence.'

'Then what exactly do you propose?' Hugh challenged him.

William turned back to look at Harold. 'You have a former neighbour who's joined the people in the Shire Wood, have you not?'

Harold nodded. 'Yeah, Ned Willows, along wiv 'is missus an' two kids — always assumin' that they 'asn't starved ter death, or bin taken up by the sheriff's men, that is.'

'Would you be allowed to pay him a visit, do you think?' William asked.

Harold's eyes opened wide momentarily, but whether in surprise or out of fear it was impossible to tell. He looked sideways at his wife Alice, but she only shrugged.

William tried pressing the point. 'Surely the people in there will recognise one of their own? And if you're bearing a few simple gifts such as clothing, beer, bread — and we can supply all those things from here — then you're more likely to be allowed to pass unmolested.'

'I dunno about that,' Harold murmured. 'Them's scared've everybody these days — even their own kind, 'cos some've 'em 'ave bin known ter peach on their neighbours, 'opin' ter keep well in wiv the sheriff. Yer askin' a lot.'

'I'm well aware of that,' William conceded, 'but if someone doesn't make the effort to break the deadlock, this sad state of affairs will just drag on forever. The people have lost faith in the justice system, and the authorities have condemned them as outlaws, rather than listening to their legitimate grievances. How many more must be starved into giving themselves up, or provoked into more violence that can only lead to the gallows? I could put a stop to all that, but I need the evidence to take to Queen Eleanor. I need to see for myself how these people live, and hear their stories from their own lips. You wouldn't just be helping your former neighbour, Harold — you'd become the local hero who brought justice back to the people of the Shire Wood.'

Alice leaned in close to Harold and muttered something in his ear. He appeared to take offence for a moment, then he nodded, although with seeming reluctance.

'Alice 'as a point. I bin shootin' me mouth off fer months about 'ow somebody ought ter do summat about the sheriff an' 'is evil ways, an' now she's tellin' me that I've got the chance ter do summat about it. I can't argue wiv Alice at the best've times, an' this time she's got a good point, like I said.'

'So you'll do it?' William asked.

Harold nodded. 'Yeah, God 'elp me. 'Ow does yer suggest I go about it?'

'You know your own business, Harold,' William replied, 'and you know both the forest and the people living in it better than I ever will. But my suggestion would be for you to go in there carrying a few gifts along the lines of those I suggested earlier, then ask to be taken to meet up with your former neighbour. Once you're there, tell them that you want to bring another man into the Shire Wood who can take steps to have the sheriff brought to justice. Don't tell them that I'm one of the

Royal Justices, because I have a feeling that it wouldn't go down well with them just at the moment.'

'Yer right there,' Harold agreed. 'An' assumin' that we gets out've there alive, yer want me ter come back an' get yer?'

'That's what I had in mind,' William nodded.

Robert spoke up for the first time. 'You won't need to. I'll go with Harold and Alice, and I can be the one to come back and guide you to where you'll find the people you need to speak to.'

'Yer not goin' wivout me!' Beth insisted as she grabbed his arm.

Robert grinned. 'Did I say I was?'

'No, but I know you, yer daft tussock! If yer went in there an' got yerself killed, I'd never speak ter yer agin.'

There was a burst of sustained laughter, provoked not only by the illogicality of Beth's threat but also relief that a difficult problem appeared to have a possible solution. More ale was passed round, and the remaining bread and cheese disappeared rapidly as everyone's appetite returned.

Once their visitors had left, and Robert and Beth had taken themselves off to supervise the hauling of logs to the sawmill, William and Hugh resumed their argument.

'Why bring me up here in the first place, if I can't lead my men in your defence when you make a foolhardy journey into an outlaw-infested forest?' Hugh protested. 'You're a lawyer, not a soldier — they'll have you trussed upside down from a convenient tree in no time at all!'

'That's the trouble with you knights,' William replied calmly. 'You think that every difference can be resolved on the point of a sword. My world is one of diplomacy and persuasion, and the last thing that these starving, homeless victims of authority need is a show of arms. They're more likely to listen to a grey-haired old man who comes among them unarmed.'

'Unarmed, and therefore defenceless,' Hugh countered. 'With respect, Father, you place a great deal of faith in your own powers of reasoning. Out there in the Holy Land, King Richard will not be sitting down with the leaders of the enemy hordes, discussing terms like reasonable, educated and courteous philosophers. They'll be hacking limbs off each other. And I return to my original point — why am I here if not to protect you, perhaps from your own rashness?'

'Your time will come, trust me,' William assured him. 'When I have the evidence I need against the sheriff, I'll need men at arms to secure his arrest. And if, as I suspect, he has the whole of Prince John's Nottingham garrison to defend him, *then* I'll have a use for your sword arm. But not before.'

Three days later the argument became irrelevant, as a dust-coated man at arms whose grimy surcoat still revealed the lions of England galloped into the manor yard, calling for Hugh at the top of his voice. Hugh appeared at the front door and recognised one of the men he'd left behind with de Coutances in London.

'Go inside and get refreshments, Ralph,' he instructed him. 'Leave your horse with me, and I'll see to its stabling.'

'It's more in need of the knacker's yard after what I've put it through the past three days,' the man answered. 'But I'll need a new one when you ride back with me to Westminster.'

'I'm needed here,' Hugh protested.

The man shook his head, regained his breath, then replied, 'You're also needed in Rouen, sir — according to the archbishop, anyway. King Philip of France has begun to attack our southern borders!'

While Hugh had been away, Richard of England — through a combination of tactical genius and sheer merciless brutality towards the enemy — had earned himself both a reputation as a great warrior and the enmity of several rival monarchs. Having overcome a massed attack by Saladin's forces at Arsuf, a day's ride from Jaffa, leaving the bones of seven thousand Muslims to bleach in the desert sun, Richard's combined force had taken Jaffa, and was creeping, day by day, closer to its goal of Jerusalem.

Then it was as if even the mighty Richard lost the impetus to keep moving forward. The weather was atrocious, unnaturally cold and wet, with hailstorms battering holes in camp canvas, and provisions becoming harder to bring down to the front line. Jerusalem was theirs for the taking, barely an hour's gallop away, but Richard hesitated, fearful that if he laid siege to the Holy City his forces would become trapped against its walls by Saladin's relief army.

Before leaving Acre for the advance across the desert to Jaffa, he'd sent a large contingent of his closest advisers as an escort for Berengaria, along with her attendants, back to the safety of Rouen, in case Saladin's army swept behind the advancing Crusaders and took them captive. He therefore had no-one upon whom to rely for tactical advice when the dispute regarding the sovereignty of Jerusalem broke out again, and Conrad of Montferrat was unanimously elected by the other Christian monarchs still present in Outremer.

The lingering dissension among these military leaders, and in particular the insistence of Henry of Champagne — the man left in charge of the French contingent following the departure of King Philip — that the Crusader army should advance on Jerusalem without further delay, proved fatal to the Christian cause. Richard attempted to negotiate with Saladin, through intermediaries, for the surrender of the city, but to no avail. Then Conrad, the newly elected ruler of a Jerusalem that was still in enemy hands, was stabbed to death in the street, and rumours began to circulate that Richard had been behind the act.

Placed in the unenviable position of being hated and distrusted by the foreign contingents of the men he was expected to lead — and faced with Saladin's stubborn refusal to yield an inch of ground — Richard ordered a full retreat back to Acre. When Saladin mounted an attack on Jaffa that was beaten back by Crusaders under Richard's command, the time was right for the Christian leader to attempt to reach an agreement with a demoralised and weakened Muslim general. The result was a three-year peace treaty under which Jerusalem would remain under Muslim control, but with unarmed Christian pilgrims and traders allowed visiting rights. Concluding, if only to himself, that he had in effect re-opened the Holy City to Christianity — and following the much-delayed receipt of despatches from his mother regarding John's suspected treachery in England — Richard set sail from Tyre in October 1192. He'd expected to be home by the spring of 1193 at the latest, but foes lay in wait for him on his long and hazardous return journey.

There were also those ill-disposed towards him closer to home. Not satisfied with the chaos and anti-royal sentiments that his brutal regime was stirring up in England, John had been making diplomatic overtures to Philip of France, who was still smarting over the insult implied by Richard's public rejection of his sister Alys. Her dowry of the Vexin had still not been returned, so Philip amassed an army and marched it north across the borders of the Île-de-France in a bid to take the Vexin back by force. When the fortress of Gisors fell without resistance, and John was invited to send English troops loyal to him to occupy the de Montfort estate at Évreux, Queen Eleanor prayed for the urgent return of Richard, and sent for Hugh of Repton to assume responsibility for the defence of Rouen in the meantime.

XVI

Robert — with Beth clinging to his arm and Harold and Alice immediately behind them, guiding the donkey whose panniers were filled with gifts — led the way up the heavily worn track that constituted the North Road. The dust that blew from under their feet with every passing step partially concealed the shabbily dressed clergyman who had been following them ever since Edwinstowe.

They were nervous and already footsore as the tower of Thoresby parish church became visible in the far distance, and Robert concluded that they had come far enough. He halted, asking, 'Isn't it about time we began shouting for this neighbour of yours, Harold? It doesn't look as if we're going to be accosted by any outlaws, who probably just take us to be ordinary farming folk making our way to or from market, so won't attempt to rob us. They're more likely to go for that monk that's been following us all morning.' He looked back down the road, then frowned. 'He's not there now — where do you think he's got to?'

'Probably went into the trees for a piss,' Harold suggested, and Robert was about to concede the point when two raggedly dressed men swished out from the undergrowth ahead of them, bearing long, sturdy staffs of what looked like oak.

'Who are yer, an' what brings yer inter the Shire Wood?' one of them demanded, as the dark-robed cleric who'd been behind them all the way suddenly stepped out from behind their two interrogators. 'Brother Paul here says as 'ow yer walked all the way from Edwinstowe, so yer likely not on the sheriff's business, but yer donkey seems well loaded. What's in its bags?'

'Me name's 'Arold Greenwood,' Harold replied in a voice made higher than usual by his nervousness, 'and I'm lookin' fer one've me old neighbours — a bloke called Ned Willows. We ain't seen 'im since 'e were driven off 'is land be the sheriff's men, an' me an' the missus — that's 'er, next ter me — thought we'd bring 'im an' 'is family some food an' clothes.'

'So who are the other two?'

'I'm Robert Repton, from the estate of that name alongside the Trent on the road from Nottingham to Lichfield,' Robert replied boldly. 'This young lady's my intended. Her name's Beth, and Alice Greenwood here is her cousin. It's our donkey, so we just came along for a day out, so to speak.'

'So 'ow come yer talks all fancy?' asked one of the men with a suspicious frown.

'Because I was educated in Repton Priory,' Robert explained. 'My father's the lord of the manor, and he wanted me to be able to take my place in local society.'

'So 'e'd be likely ter pay a tidy sum fer yer ransom, that right?' the other man demanded.

Robert did his best to hide his apprehension and opted for defiance. '*He* might, but I doubt if my older brother would agree to that. He's a knight who serves King Richard, and he's currently back home in the manor house. He's more likely to run a sword through your guts than pay any ransom.'

'Brave talk fer a young squirt what's not even armed,' the second man grinned. 'Yer might be more use where we're gunna be takin' yer. It just so 'appens that I knows where Ned Willows can be found, so foller me. But if yer lyin', it'll be the worse fer yer — we doesn't like sheriff's ferrets around these parts.'

They were led down one forest track after another, further into the deepening gloom, the early afternoon sun barely visible through the canopy of the late autumn trees. They came to the crossing of two paths, and one of their guides gave a loud whistle that was answered in kind from somewhere high in a tree above them. Then they were blindfolded and led, holding hands, down what seemed to be a long slope before they reached a destination they could smell well before they reached it.

The blindfolds were removed, to reveal a camp of sorts, with rickety huts consisting of upright tree branches, over which were draped assorted animal skins in an attempt to keep out the elements. A fire was burning fitfully in the centre of the clearing, around which several filth-smeared children sat staring up at the new arrivals, while suspicious adult eyes surveyed them from within the shaded awnings of the crude dwellings.

One of their captors called out loudly for Ned Willows, and a skeletally thin man with a pronounced stoop emerged from one of the huts, blinking against the light.

'D'yer recognise any o' these folk?' he was asked.

Ned looked blankly at the group for a moment, then replied, 'Ain't that 'Arold Greenwood an' 'is missus? They looks like I remembers 'em, anyroad. I don't know who the other two might be.'

'It's us, right enough,' Harold called back, 'and we've brought yer some food an' some've Alice's crab-apple cider, along wiv a few coneys fer the pot. There's some clothes an' all.'

Shortly after sunset, they were watching the coney grease spurting into the fire from the crude metal spit laid across it. The plump rabbits had been skinned and gutted by Ned's wife.

'So how are things, living rough here in the Shire Wood?' Robert asked politely.

Ned eyed him suspiciously. 'What's it ter you?'

'My father's the lord of the manor of Repton, west of Nottingham, and he didn't find it necessary to evict any of his tenants — unlike the sheriff who turned out all those folk like yourself living in the Shire Wood. Our tenants couldn't pay their term rents any more than you could, but he allowed them to stay on with their debts suspended until better times, which of course have now begun.'

Ned spat into the fire. 'The rents was just an excuse. The sheriff were told ter clear all the land 'e could, fer Prince John's huntin've the deer. We'd taken ter killin' 'em ourselves, yer see, ter feed our families when the 'arvest were poor.'

'But we heard that when evicting the tenants who were in arrears, the sheriff and his men employed brutal methods that were themselves against the law.'

'So bloody what?' Ned demanded with resignation. 'At the end've the day, the sheriff can do whatever 'e likes ter peasants like us, can't 'e?'

'Not by law he can't,' Robert insisted.

Ned gave him a long, hard look. 'An' what does *you* know about the law, then?'

'There are people who'd like to see the sheriff held to account for his wicked deeds.'

'People what's got an army, yer mean?' Ned asked sarcastically.

Robert nodded. 'Precisely. I have a brother who fights alongside King Richard, and he'd come down very hard on your sheriff if he were to learn what he's been up to during the king's absence on Crusade.'

'That's just the point, though,' Ned argued back. 'As long as the king's on that there Crusade, 'e can't do owt ter 'elp the like've us, can 'e?'

'Perhaps not him in person, but my father is very friendly with a Royal Justice who can, and who would be supported in his actions by King Richard upon his return.'

'An' 'ow der we know that yer've not bin sent by the sheriff yerself, ter trick us inter sayin' summat that'd get us 'ung?'

'He can't get at you deep in the Shire Wood here, can he?' Robert reasoned. 'Even if I *was* one of the sheriff's men, I could never find my way back here, so where's the risk to you?'

'So why are yer *really* 'ere?' Ned demanded.

'I want to be allowed to bring my father here, so that he can hear all your stories, and report them back to Queen Eleanor, who's looking after the nation until Richard returns. Then he'll be able to contact his friend the Royal Justice, and have the sheriff arrested.'

'I'll need ter ask permission,' Ned told him.

'By all means,' Robert agreed. 'It looks as if we'll have to stay the night here anyway, so by morning you can let us have your answer.'

After the coneys, black bread and cider had been disposed of by Ned, his family and a few families in nearby lean-to huts like their own, Robert and Beth made their bed in the shade of a spreading oak, covered by an evil-smelling deer hide. Harold and Alice crawled under the overhang of Ned's hut.

Robert was almost on the point of dozing off when he caught a murmured conversation between Ned, who'd remained by the dying embers of the fire, and one of the men who'd ordered their party off the North Road. He didn't quite catch the first part of the conversation, but he clearly heard the words that followed.

'Robin says it's worth the risk, but if yer bein' tricked, yer on yer own.'

XVII

'You took your time about it,' de Coutances complained when Hugh presented himself inside the chancellor's ground-floor chamber in Westminster. 'You're to lose no time in returning to Rouen, and please God you're not too late already. You should be able to get there in three days, depending on the tides from Dover and the fitness of your horse.'

'But you could never keep up with me, with respect,' Hugh pointed out as tactfully as he could. 'Do you want me to ride on ahead?'

'I won't be coming with you,' de Coutances grimaced. 'I have too much to do here, holding things together. Much has been happening here in England during your sojourn in the countryside.'

'But I am to travel to Rouen to defend it against Philip of France? Has he returned from the Crusade?'

'The Crusade has been abandoned, or so we hear, and all the kings who committed their forces to it are said to be returning. It seems that Philip left them some months ago, and has been stirring trouble for England as a result of Richard's foolhardy decision to cast aside Princess Alys and marry that woman from Navarre.'

'That was as much his mother's decision as anyone's,' Hugh told him. 'But if King Richard is returning to us, why am I so urgently needed in Rouen? Not that I'm complaining, since I have certain interests of the heart to pursue, and of course my mother is there, attending Queen Dowager Eleanor. But what has been happening here in my absence?'

De Coutances sighed heavily and gestured for Hugh to take a seat. 'First, you must be advised that de Longchamp is no longer Chancellor of England, nor is he a justiciar. In fact, he is no longer in England.'

'He has been dismissed from office and exiled?'

'Dismissed from office certainly, but it was his decision to flee the country. It is feared that he may be seeking sanctuary in Paris.'

'What awful events led to that, pray?'

'You may recall that Richard and John have a half-brother — a bastard son of the former King Henry — who was consecrated Archbishop of York, but who undertook to remain out of the country for as long as Richard was on Crusade?'

'Yes, of course. The fear was that he might make an alliance with Prince John.'

'Precisely. Well, in breach of that undertaking he returned in secret to Dover, where he was however recognised by its castellan, who alerted de Longchamp. Realising that he was discovered, he took sanctuary in a nearby priory, but de Longchamp gave orders for him to be removed from there and imprisoned.'

'In Richard's best interests, surely? Wherein lies the fault in that?'

'Violation of sanctuary?' de Coutances reminded him, open-mouthed. 'Have you learned nothing from your lawyer father? It is a most grievous action, and one that offends both the law of the land and the Church. To make matters worse, Geoffrey was seemingly dragged out by his arms and legs while he was at prayer before the altar at which he had been conducting Mass for the Holy Brothers. This came too close to the memory of what happened to Becket barely two decades ago, and Prince

John called a meeting of the council at which I was powerless to prevent the fool from being removed from office and indicted for his assault upon the Primate of England. He fled abroad, and while in London John took the opportunity to make himself agreeable to the people there by granting them self-government under a mayor.'

'Then de Puiset remains as sole Justiciar of England?'

'He does indeed. We may confidently expect him to demonstrate his gratitude to John in many ways, both as Justiciar and as Bishop of Durham. Even now they are touring the nation in some sort of triumphant progress, with John presiding over his own courts and distributing largesse and other favours to leading barons. He is also putting it abroad that Richard named him as his heir while on Crusade, and that he will never return from Outremer, so it is in England's best interests that John be proclaimed king without delay.'

Hugh sat stunned by all this bad news, then asked, 'Has all this been made known to Queen Eleanor?'

'Indeed it has, and she has formally appointed me as head of the Regency Council, for all the use that is. She remains in Rouen, where she has now been rejoined by Queen Berengaria and her lady. Meanwhile, there are rumours that John intends to journey to Paris. He claims that he is pursuing de Longchamp, but those who report to me from within John's retinue believe that it is his intention to sign a treaty with Philip of France.'

'I had almost forgotten why you summoned me here in the first place,' said Hugh. 'Rouen is feared to be under threat of attack from Philip?'

'We cannot be certain, of course, but Gisors fell to him without a blow being struck, and we believe that John may be prevailed upon to take occupation of Évreux, in the heart of the Vexin. This was Princess Alys's dowry, you may recall, and Richard has thus far declined to hand it back. But we fear that Philip will not settle for retaking the Vexin, but will, under John's urgings, push further north into Normandy.'

'I can now see clearly why I need to rally the defences at Rouen,' said Hugh, but de Coutances shook his head.

'That is not why I summoned you. One more sword — even one as skilfully wielded as yours — would make little difference. The key to preserving our estates in Normandy lies in blocking John's plans to pledge allegiance to Philip of France. John is still in England, and we believe that the timely return of Queen Eleanor might prevent his departure. Your task is to secure her safe return, along with the other ladies in her party, including Queen Berengaria, who has yet to set foot in her husband's land. But what of your father's enquiries into any provable misdeeds by John? Has he made progress?'

'I believe so,' Hugh replied. 'As I left he was making plans to visit a place called the "Shire Wood", north of Nottingham, which is one of John's preferred hunting grounds. There have allegedly been many foul deeds committed by the sheriff in whose domain this wood lies, designed to clear the forest of those who currently reside in it, and there are grounds for believing that those atrocities were committed on John's instruction. If so, then we may be able to bring at least the sheriff to trial, while revealing to the nation at large that Prince John is not the peoples' friend that he would have folks believe.'

'Let us hope that your father does not meet with treachery,' de Coutances murmured. 'He is no soldier like yourself.'

'I attempted to reason with him, but he would not let me act as his protector when he eventually meets with those who can provide the evidence against the sheriff, assuming that he does. We were still arguing that point when I was summoned south.'

'And now you know why. Lose no time in journeying to Rouen and bringing back the one woman who can perhaps preserve the nation ahead of the welcome return of its rightful king.'

The Channel crossing was turbulent, as was usual for late autumn, and Hugh was glad to be reunited with his land legs as he rode hard from Boulogne, deep in thought. His elation at the prospect of being reunited with Edwina was tempered by the depressing news he'd received regarding John's growing ambitions in Richard's absence. Even though he knew that his father had sometimes argued with de Longchamp, at least they had both been committed to preserving the nation while Richard pursued his ill-advised dreams of reconquering the Holy Land for Rome. Now John had been able to manoeuvre de Longchamp out of office, and he'd clearly made a fawning lackey out of the only remaining justiciar, de Puiset. Even worse seemed to be de Longchamp's betrayal as he sought sanctuary from Philip of France.

The spires of Rouen eventually came into sight at noon on the third day of a very tiring ride, and Hugh rode into the stable yard and dismounted. He enquired as to where Queen Eleanor might be found as a groom took his horse's bridle.

'I believe her to be taking the morning air in the rose walk, along with her ladies,' the groom replied. 'Shall I have you announced?'

'No, thank you,' Hugh replied with a smile. 'I believe they are expecting me, and I no longer require leave to approach the presence.'

He walked out of the stable courtyard and through the gap in the curtain wall of the upper keep that led into the perfumed rose garden. In the distance he spotted the somewhat hesitant, and slightly stooped, figure of Eleanor with Adele holding her arm, perhaps as much for her own stability as her mistress's. Rather than cause them any alarm by approaching unannounced, he called out. Both women turned.

Adele said something to Eleanor, in reply to which Eleanor nodded. Adele then scurried over as quickly as her ageing legs permitted and threw her arms around her son as she enquired after his father.

'Well enough when last I saw him, but you will shortly be reunited, since I am commissioned to take Queen Eleanor back to England. I assume that Queen Berengaria will also be paying her first visit to her new realm?'

Adele's face clouded briefly as she shook her head. 'She has asked to be allowed to remain here, to await King Richard's return. His chaplain, Hubert Walter, has been back for two weeks now, and we expect Richard any day. For that reason we may delay our departure, in order to reunite mother, son and wife. Talking of which, you may rest assured that Lady Edwina remains in good health. She and Berengaria returned from the Holy Land free of any disease, God be praised.'

'I had hoped that they would be here, walking with your mistress.'

'Berengaria has a slight chill, and as for Edwina, she has other reasons for remaining within her chamber. You must come with me.'

Slightly puzzled, Hugh made a show of bowing respectfully to Eleanor as she stood smiling at him from the far end of the rose walk. He then allowed his mother to guide him into the castle, and up a flight of stairs to the private entrance to the royal apartments. Halfway down, Hugh remembered, was the withdrawing chamber that was no doubt now occupied by England's new queen, and on the far side of that the next door gave access to the chamber of the senior lady, who was now Edwina.

He was therefore a little taken aback when Adele led him to the third door down, and tapped gently on it before pushing it open. Inside he could see the figure of a middle-aged palace servant hunched over a bed, and his heart leaped to his mouth with the thought that Edwina might be ill.

He turned and looked back at his mother, who smiled and urged him to approach the bed. As he did so he made a subconscious note that it was smaller than average, then realised that it must in fact be a child's nursery cot. The servant bowed her head out of respect then moved to one side, and Hugh looked down at the sleeping form of a baby less than a year old, with a head of soft black hair.

He turned back towards the doorway, and there stood Edwina, looking both happy and apprehensive as she locked eyes with him.

'I hope you don't mind, but I had him christened "Geoffrey",' she said. 'It goes very well with "Repton", does it not?'

'You mean it's mine?' Hugh asked, open-mouthed.

Edwina pouted. 'No — he's *ours*. Don't you *dare* insult me by suggesting otherwise, or I won't agree to marry you, and that delightful gift from God will be adjudged a bastard all his days.'

'But — I mean, *how?*' Hugh mumbled.

Edwina chuckled. 'How do you think? Was it such an ordinary event for you that you've already forgotten it?'

'Of *course* I haven't! Look, forgive me, but this is a bit of a surprise.'

She left the doorway and scurried into his arms. 'Do you like him?'

'Well, he seems pleasant enough from what I've seen so far, and he has my dark hair.'

'Stop teasing!' she grinned as she kissed him. 'Isn't he just the most beautiful thing you ever saw?'

'Apart from his mother, yes,' Hugh replied. 'Where was he born?'

'Tyre. I didn't realise that I was expecting until after you'd returned to England. I'd had a few strange bodily sensations that we needn't go into, and my maidenly events had not occurred for several months, but I took those to be the effects of that awful shipwreck. Then when my mistress caught me vomiting into an empty serving bowl, she insisted that I consult the surgeon who was in attendance on Richard's army. He advised me — rather rudely, I thought — that none of his men had ever exhibited such symptoms, and he arranged for a local physician to examine me. The same physician attended my lying-in, and it wasn't nearly as bad as other women claim. But then, the Arab physicians are said to be finest in the world, are they not?'

'What was the reaction of the other women in your party here?'

'Well, as you would expect, your mother began to cluck like a mother hen. Some days, it's a contest to see which of us will get to his cot first when he wakes in the morning. Usually it's your mother, since he's taken to waking at night, and then sometimes the wet nurse has to hand him to me, because only my milk will satisfy him. On those nights I often sleep for longer, and sometimes I'm late for my duties. As for my mistress, she's been very understanding, and has assigned other ladies to the more physical duties such as robing her, although she still insists that I dress her hair. The only one who seems to be indifferent to Geoffrey is Queen Eleanor, but then she has a good number of other matters to occupy her attention.'

'That's why I'm here,' Hugh told her. 'We're all going back to England, to try to put a stop to Prince John's attempts to seize the throne while King Richard's still in the Holy Land, although I heard tell that he's on his way home. I assume that he'll come by way of Rouen, but we need to cross the Channel to England without delay.'

'Can we get married first?'

'If you can secure the services of a suitable priest, then of course,' Hugh said. 'Although we have already made the pledge before God that really matters.'

'I agree, but "Geoffrey the Bastard" would not be a good name for our firstborn to carry through life.'

'It was good enough for the current Archbishop of York,' Hugh replied, 'although he was the bastard of a king, so perhaps that was different. However, de Longchamp lost his appointment as Chancellor and Justiciar by opposing his return to England, in breach of his oath to Richard to stay away.'

'No more talk of courtly affairs,' Edwina urged him. 'Instead, let's go and find Queen Eleanor's confessor — the Bishop of Salisbury, as it transpires — and ask if he still remembers how to conduct a marriage ceremony.'

'I'll need a few days to organise things, such as a witness on my side,' Hugh told her. 'Then there's the matter of your dowry.'

Edwina tapped his nose playfully. 'You didn't ask what I was worth when you bedded me, but my father is the Earl of Flint, and I'm his only child. So you may one day inherit a large expanse of nothing in particular to the north-west of Chester, positioned by the sea on a shore that is so windy that the birds often fly backwards.'

Hugh chuckled, took her hand and led her to the chamber door. As they passed through it they came cross Adele, lurking in the corridor.

'At least you agreed to do the decent thing and marry the poor girl,' she smiled at Hugh. 'Now, dearest Edwina, is it my turn with the baby? And by the way, Hugh, Queen Eleanor wishes to speak with you once you are free. I think she meant free of Edwina's grip.'

Hugh answered Eleanor's summons a short while later.

'Congratulations on becoming a father,' Eleanor said without any obvious warmth. 'It will give you greater incentive to remain here.'

'I thought I was required to escort you back across the Channel with all speed,' he objected.

She shook her head. 'You are to remain here to guard Queen Berengaria, who does not wish to enter England except by Richard's side. Since she will require the Lady Edwina to attend her, it is fitting that you remain in charge of the Palace Guard, given the rumours of King Philip's plans to invade Normandy.'

'Then who will escort you safely back to England, Your Highness?'

'We have recently been joined by a man you have no doubt come across during your time in my son's army. The Earl of Pembroke?'

'William Marshall? I took him to still be on his way back from Crusade.'

'He returned with Hubert Walter, the Bishop of Salisbury, who acted as Richard's chaplain. All of which begs the question of what has delayed Richard's own return, but whatever that may be, Berengaria would prefer to await him here, and William Marshall will be a more than adequate protector for what should be a safe enough passage to Portsmouth.'

'Not Dover, Your Highness?'

'No, because John is said to be riding to Southampton, ahead of taking ship to travel by way of Caen, thus avoiding us here at Rouen. We should lose no time in departing, if we are to cut him off before he sails.'

'I was hoping that the bishop might agree to marry Edwina and myself.'

Eleanor nodded. 'I'm sure he'd be agreeable, and not before time. But make it within the next day or so.'

XVIII

Two days later, Hugh and Edwina became man and wife, with Berengaria standing as Edwina's witness while William Marshall performed the same service for his former military comrade. Standing slightly behind them was the proud grandmother Adele, nursing little Geoffrey, who slept contentedly in her arms throughout the brief service.

They had just reached the 'sweets' stage of the wedding banquet when a page entered the Great Hall and whispered something in Eleanor's ear. She nodded, and a minute later the same page announced the hurried entrance of Walter de Coutances. He ignored the rest of the company as he strode purposefully to Eleanor's side and spoke to her in hushed tones. She turned pale and clutched at the rosary that always hung round her neck as she murmured, 'God help us!' She then rose and ran from the hall, her hand to her mouth, followed closely behind by Adele, who reappeared a few moments later to call for Hugh and William Marshall to attend upon Eleanor.

As they entered the side chamber together, it was obvious to both men that the news was grave, and very personal to Eleanor, who sat ashen-faced and shaking. Adele was attempting to persuade her to drink a little wine.

De Coutances beckoned Hugh and Marshall to one side and whispered hoarsely, 'King Richard has been taken prisoner, and there are fears for his life!'

An hour later, when Eleanor had taken to her bed, de Coutances explained in more detail as they sat before the fire in the Audience Chamber.

'I am fortunate to have in my pay a most assiduous clerk who is employed at the French court, for whom I was once able to perform a great service that preserved his soul from the Hell that awaits all such sinners. From him I obtained, by way of a messenger who serves the de Montforts on their estate within the Île-de-France, the copy of a letter sent by the Holy Roman Emperor to Philip of France. Have I already succeeded in losing you?'

'Not me,' Marshall growled. 'I had occasion to cross lances with that pig's bladder Henry of Germany during a tournament in Neuenburg as part of the treaty negotiations between his father and Henry of Saxony, who is of course married to King Richard's sister Matilda.'

'The two Henrys have remained enemies for many years,' de Coutances added, 'but recently Henry of Germany became Holy Roman Emperor, and in his triumph he has set about settling many old scores. Among those who hide behind him is Leopold of Austria, who has hated Richard with a passion since he pulled his battle banner from the walls of Acre and trod it into the dirt.'

'I saw nothing of that, of course,' Hugh reminded him, 'because I was ordered to accompany Queen Eleanor and my mother back here, along with the royal sister Joan.'

'There was even more than that,' Marshall added glumly. 'When Conrad of Montferrat was murdered in a back street of Jaffa, it was popularly rumoured that Richard's had been the hand behind it. Conrad was cousin to Leopold of Austria.'

'So how has the king come to be a prisoner?' Hugh asked anxiously.

De Coutances, with a darkened expression, went on, 'It seems that having departed from Acre he was bound for Marseille, but was overtaken by a storm like the one that beset his fleet on the outward journey, and after many hardships he found himself cast ashore near Slovenia. He was by that stage thoroughly disenchanted with sea travel and decided to come home by way of Austria and Germany, and from thence into France. But despite donning a disguise he was recognised by one of the vassals of Duke Leopold, and taken prisoner. Leopold was all for killing him and throwing his body into the Danube, but wiser counsels prevailed and instead he had him transferred to a castle in Dürnstein. He then informed his cousin the Holy Roman Emperor of his valuable captive.'

'He is still alive?' Hugh asked anxiously.

'He is, but Henry of Germany informed Philip of France of Richard's capture, and between them they have hidden him away — we know not where. It is feared that they will do him to death.'

'Philip will no doubt seek to use Richard's delayed return to invade Normandy through the Vexin,' Marshall added gloomily. 'It's a pity that Queen Eleanor wishes for me to return to England with her, because I may well be needed to take a force south and ensure that the *seigneur* of Évreux remains loyal.'

'Given his family connections with England, it's hardly likely he'll defect to Philip,' Hugh observed with more confidence than he felt. 'And you may safely leave the defence of Normandy to me.'

'I meant no disrespect,' Marshall said, 'but we must clearly take what steps we can to secure the safety of all our lands until Richard's release.'

'I can send envoys to the courts of both France and Germany,' de Coutances suggested. 'It may be that they seek merely a ransom — God forbid that they wish us to yield the Vexin, or some of our fortresses to the south of Normandy.'

'Is there no friendly — or at least neutral — monarch to whom we can turn in order to intercede on our behalf for Richard's release?' Marshall asked de Coutances, who nodded vigorously.

'Now you put me in mind of the matter, the imprisonment of a Crusader king is in violation of the "Truce of God", as the Pope called it when giving the enterprise his blessing. I shall lose no time in drafting a formal protest to him.'

'It was Pope Gregory who proclaimed the Crusade originally,' Marshall reminded him. 'We are on our third Pope since then — think you that Pope Celestine will be prepared to enforce the "Truce"?'

'A papal bull is a papal bull,' de Coutances replied. 'The "Truce of God" specifically forbade one crusading monarch from proceeding in any way against the interests of another during their absence. If future ordinances of this kind are to be seen to have any authority, then successive Popes are obliged to uphold what came before. You may recall the bull issued by the former Pope Gregory that declared the Church of Rome to be free of constraints from secular authority. Think you that any subsequent Pope would seek to resile from that?'

'We can but try,' Hugh observed, 'but is there nothing of a more practical nature that we should be turning our minds to?'

'The governance of England in the immediate future,' Marshall replied sternly. 'Queen Eleanor has graciously conferred regency powers on me, and I am to join her council once we land back on English shores. Then it will be a matter of ensuring that Prince John does not seek to use Richard's absence in order to take over the throne.'

'My father was embarked on a similar venture,' Hugh told them. 'He was, in his capacity as a Royal Justice, concerned to learn of certain violations of law that were occurring in the vicinity of our estate in Derbyshire, by the hand of the local sheriff. He'd also come across similar misdeeds in York, but had been prevented from proceeding against them by Justiciar de Puiset, who he believed to also be in John's pay. When I was summoned back to London, he was preparing to seek out evidence of John's malfeasance in the Royal Forest that adjoins Nottingham Castle, in the hope of persuading Chancellor de Longchamp to proceed upon it.'

'This may explain why John pressed so hard for de Longchamp's dismissal from office,' de Coutances said grimly. 'There is clearly a network of corruption of office lurking beneath the surface in the land that Richard so unwisely left in the wrong hands, being too trusting of his treacherous younger brother. This merely reinforces my original thought that the sooner we leave Rouen the better. Eleanor has commanded Marshall to accompany us, while Hugh takes command of Rouen, and — if necessary — the defence of the whole of Normandy. We shall all need God's protection if we are to ensure the safe return of England to a peaceful state under its rightful king. In furtherance of which, I shall write to the Pope this very day.'

By the time that Eleanor's party rode out of Rouen, the Pope had reacted angrily to what he had been advised of by de Coutances, and had excommunicated Leopold of Austria, while threatening to place the whole of King Philip's lands under interdict if he set one foot on English land north of the

Île-de-France. But this did not of itself result in Richard's release, and it was with a heavy heart that Eleanor saw the entrance to Portsmouth Sound coming closer from where she sat in the stern of the vessel that had conveyed her and her party from Le Havre. There were several vessels behind hers filled with English knights and their horses returning from the Crusade, and on the quayside they were met by a further detachment of Westminster Palace guards, led by their captain, John Maltravers.

'Prince John is still in Southampton, Your Majesty,' Maltravers told her with a gallant bow. 'May I welcome you back on our shores, and be granted the honour of accompanying you thence?'

'You may,' Eleanor replied as she was escorted to the litter that awaited her. 'And you may see to it that my imminent arrival is announced in whichever whorehouse my son may be located, and that John is left in no doubt that his mother is not pleased.'

Two hours later, John and his immediate retinue were waiting outside St Mary's Church. The queen's entourage swept into its spacious forecourt and formed a semi-circle in front of John's vastly outnumbered company. He stepped swiftly forward to assist Eleanor from her litter, but she glared at him disapprovingly and deliberately held out her hand instead to William Marshall. 'Offer me your hand when it does not contain a serpent,' she told John.

'Mother?'

'Do not seek to address me as "Mother" until you have ceased seeking ways to undermine my authority.'

'In what ways is it said that I have done that?' John asked. 'Name the man and I shall have him done to death.'

'Without a trial, as seems to be your normal mode of procedure? I have heard much of the way you conduct the affairs of England in your brother's absence, and none of it does you any credit.'

'You misjudge me, Mother,' John protested.

Eleanor maintained her disdainful stare as she asked, 'What are you doing in Southampton?'

'Inspecting the fleet, ahead of launching an attack on Philip of France, who I am advised is holding Richard prisoner. We have received a request for his ransom that England has no hope of raising, and I shall be invading France in order to secure the release of my beloved brother.'

'He would be dead long before you reached the Vexin, as you are well aware,' Eleanor snapped. 'As for the English fleet, unless my old eyes deceived me, I passed it in Portsmouth. So I ask again — why are you in Southampton?'

When this elicited no response, Eleanor fired another question at him.

'How much is this ransom, and what steps have you taken to raise the money?'

'The Treasury, as you know, was left empty after Richard stripped it for his Crusade,' John replied evasively, 'added to which, a series of poor harvests resulted in a shortfall of the revenues we might ordinarily expect. I have ordered a tithe on both secular estates and Church properties, but even then it will be a long time before we can raise the one hundred and fifty thousand marks that are being demanded.'

There was a stunned silence, during which William Marshall took a firmer hold of Eleanor's elbow as he felt her sag at the knees. She finally found her voice, but there was still a quaver in it as she replied assertively, 'Perhaps *you* cannot stir yourself sufficiently to raise such a sum for the release of your brother, but I most certainly can for the life of my son. We shall ride immediately to London and begin the process.'

'I shall accompany you,' John offered, to be rewarded with a derisive snort.

'Think you that you had a choice? You are fortunate that you will do so on your own horse, and not tied behind another, to walk for the entire four days. That at least would have been a better use of your time than a token attack on the king who holds your brother's life in his hands. Let us away, and hopefully we shall see the spires of Winchester before nightfall.'

XIX

'It was somewhere around here, just as we caught sight of Thoresby up ahead,' Robert told William in a muted voice as they stared into the dense foliage. They had ridden from Repton at daybreak, and the sun was now high overhead as they sauntered casually up the North Road, hoping that Robert would be recognised from his foray into the outlaw camp two weeks previously. It was also to be hoped that Robert's promise to bring back a man who was committed to seeking justice for their cause would also be recalled, and they would not be set upon and robbed as if they were ordinary travellers. William had taken care not to dress too richly for the occasion, but even so his saddle and other accoutrements might seem attractive to a starving beggar.

They barely had time to comprehend what was happening before there was sudden movement to their left, and a giant of a man pulled William clean off his horse, carrying him into the adjacent shrubbery. Another man had Robert similarly restrained, and they were carried half a mile into the forest before the huge man dropped William to the ground, knelt on his back and tied his wrists together. The same fate befell Robert, then they were ordered to their feet and each tied to a sturdy young oak tree.

'That should keep them where we want them,' the giant told his companion. 'Now lose no time in alerting Robin, while I stand guard.'

Shortly after their capture, a smiling man slipped out from a clump of bracken with the stealth of a deer. His progress was all but obscured by the green and brown tunic and hose that he was sporting. 'I must apologise for the rough manner of your welcome,' he said. 'We cannot be too careful about who we allow to visit our humble company, but I am advised by one of your captors that the younger man has been here before, and promised to return with someone who could be of assistance to us.' He nodded towards William. 'You, I assume, are that man?'

'I am indeed,' William replied, 'but I would be able to speak more freely if my hands were not tied behind this tree.'

The man smiled and ordered his two henchmen to untie their captives, then pointed down the broad pathway through the five-foot high bracken. 'Please join us for our midday meal. While we are becoming a little tired of venison, you perhaps may find it to your liking, particularly since it once belonged to Prince John, for whom I am advised you have little regard.'

Thirty minutes or so later, they came to a broad clearing where the undergrowth had been cleared in order to make room for what looked like any country village to be encountered in that deeply forested part of England. There were several sturdily built cottages with thatched roofs, a huddle of storage sheds, and livestock tethered to various stakes in the soil. Women were tending cooking pots over fires lit on the bare earth in the centre of the clearing, while children were either toying with homemade hoops or engaging in acrobatic feats of various types. Their host bid them seat themselves on the ground, and a well-groomed lady of approximately the same age as him served them with ale in wooden pots that appeared to have been hand carved from tree branches.

'Now, before we raise a toast to the brewer whose wagon supplied this excellent ale on its way to the royal hunting lodge, your name, if you would be so obliging?' said their host.

'I'm William, Earl of Repton in South Derbyshire. I have an estate there, and this is my son Robert, who manages the estate.'

Their host smiled. 'I *thought* that we might be entertaining someone of substance, like I once was. I too had an estate — in my case on the other side of the forest here, when I was "Robert of Swinecote". Swinecote ceased to be mine when I was obliged to escape what passes for the guardians of law and order in this part of the country.'

'Am I allowed to know why?' William asked.

'I killed one of the sheriff's men.'

'Sheriff de Wendenal?'

'Is there any other? But why do you not enquire *why* I killed the man?'

William smiled. 'Because I have no doubt of two things; the first is that you probably had just cause, and the second is that you are about to tell me anyway.'

The man grimaced. 'The sheriff turned up on the estate with several of his henchmen, insisting that all my tenants be evicted immediately because I had not paid what was alleged to be a levy in compensation for the loss of several deer from the royal hunting lodge at Clipstone. That is close to my former estate of Swinecote, and I suspected that the venison had indeed been taken by some of my tenants, as the king's verderer was alleging. However, I was not about to voice my suspicions, lest those who had done what they did only to preserve their families from starvation were roasted over an open fire in full view of the other tenants, as seems to be Sheriff de Wendenal's preferred method of extracting retribution.'

'But they went ahead with the evictions anyway?' William guessed.

The man nodded. 'Brutally, of course.'

'And you lost control of your normally mild humour and killed a man?'

'I did indeed, in a moment of cold rage when I saw him set fire to the cottage of an elderly widow who was lying inside, bed-ridden and close to death. I can still hear her screams on nights when I sleep poorly.'

'And then you ran away and hid here? How long ago was that?'

'Almost two years now, at the end of that long period of poor harvests.'

'You were declared an outlaw?'

'I was indeed, along with my wife and children, in accordance with a practice whose lawfulness I would challenge, were I able. As it is, we dwell here in humbled circumstances, living off what we can catch or steal. As you can see, there are many more like me. The lady who served your beer was my wife, Matilda, although she now calls herself "Marion", in case any of those by whom we are surrounded are captured and tortured.'

'I heard reference to a leader of this band called "Robin",' William recalled. 'Would that by any chance be *your* adopted name, since you advise me that your birth name was "Robert"?'

'Correct,' Robin said. 'We all use assumed names, for the reasons I already advanced. The large man who tied you to a tree — for which I apologise once again — is John Nailer, from Hathersage in the north of Derbyshire. He has adopted the somewhat ironic new identity of "Little John".'

'Ironic indeed,' William chuckled. 'He must be seven feet in height, and he lifted me bodily out of my saddle!'

'He has his gentler side,' Robin grinned. 'Your horses, by the way, are being taken care of, and will be available to you when you depart.'

'We *shall* be allowed to depart?' Robert asked, as his first contribution to the conversation.

Robin looked faintly offended. 'Do we strike you as cut-throats or idle vagabonds?'

'Indeed not,' William assured him, 'although there is much talk of your robbing travellers on the North Road.'

'Also along what is known as "The King's Great Way", but only the wealthy ones,' Robin explained, 'and unless they stand and fight, they are never harmed. But we have to survive somehow, as do those less fortunate even than ourselves, to whom we regularly pass on the wealth we have acquired. This way, our community is more evenly allocated the essentials of life. We have obviously learned to live by our wits, and have considerably honed our skills in archery, swordplay, hunting and stalking. But we were once all peaceful men minding our own business, tilling the land, tending our crops or following our trades. We even have our own attendant clergyman, Brother Paul, a friar from Hucknall who now delights in the name of "Friar Huck". As for the others, let me see if I can demonstrate my point.'

He called out various names, and an assortment of men, dressed in the same brown and green apparel that made them almost invisible in a forest environment, sauntered over to where the three of them sat watching the venison cooking over the fire pit. Robin effected the introductions.

'This man is Alan, from Stanton Dale, who is still one of the finest bow-makers in the north of the country. He has put his skills to good use under his assumed name of "Alan of the Dale". Similarly the red-faced man, whose somewhat terrifying new name of "Hugh Meathanger" barely disguises his former trade as a butcher in Shirebrook, has skills we call upon whenever we fell a deer. He came here in the company of a dyer from neighbouring Scarcliffe — who as William Dyer clothed some of the wealthy upon whom he now preys as "Will Scarlet", named after the cloth hue he was always seeking to perfect. The older man to the rear of the group was the operator of the Ollerton grain mill that was burned to the ground when he refused to grind corn free of charge for the hunting lodge, and he now makes bread for us as "Much the Miller". Finally, there is the man we call "Peterkin", who as Peter from Somercotes deserted the sheriff's service when he refused to mutilate yet another child whose father could not produce a quarter rent. There are many more, but as you can see they were once adjudged honest men. They still are, but now they carry the yoke of outlawry around their necks.'

'And their stories shall all be told,' William assured him as he accepted several slices of piping hot venison served to him by the lady calling herself Marion.

'Told to whom?' Robin asked.

William realised that he would need to go about the next part of his business in easy stages. 'I have not been entirely honest with you all,' he admitted, 'to the extent that I did not reveal my full rank. I am indeed William of Repton, and an earl through the generosity of the late King Henry, whose son Richard I now serve. But I did not also reveal that King Richard, in his generosity, appointed me as a King's Justice.'

Robin stared at him with a mixture of disbelief, shock and embarrassment, then finally mumbled, 'Forgive me my coarse handling of you both on your arrival. I had no idea, obviously, and I seek forgiveness once again for such rudery to a king's man.'

'There is no need for forgiveness,' William said reassuringly, 'and I only mention my office in order to advise you, with what hopefully will be persuasion, that the person who shall hear of the way you have been mistreated, and your current plight, is Queen Eleanor.'

'She is still in life?'

'She is indeed, and when last I heard she was residing in Rouen, which is in Normandy. Her son King Richard is currently on Crusade in the Holy Land, attended by my son Hugh. I have heard much of Prince John's wickedness in his brother's absence, and it is my intention to report all I have learned to the Chief Justiciar, Walter de Coutances. He will report it in due course to Queen Eleanor, and I shall return here armed with warrants for the arrest of Sheriff de Wendenal.'

'I wish you good luck and God speed in that, my friend,' Robin smiled broadly as he reached out to shake William's hand. 'You must stay here this night, and then on the morrow some of my men will see you safely back to Repton. And should you require the services of some of the best archers in England, you need only call.'

Barely three days after their landing at Portsmouth, most of the new Regency Council that Eleanor had summoned as a matter of urgency were gathered around the long table in the Council Chamber on the ground floor of Westminster Palace. Eleanor sat at its head, with Adele seated in a window alcove to the side, in case her mistress required anything.

Down the table sat those who were deemed by the queen dowager to be the most important to England at this critical time: Walter de Coutances, William Marshall, Richard FitzNigel, Bishop of London, Hubert Walter, shortly to be anointed as the new Archbishop of Canterbury, the Earls of Arundel and Surrey and Henry FitzAilwin, the first elected Mayor of London under the freedom charter granted by the noticeably absent Prince John.

There was only one item of business, and Eleanor lost no time in broaching it.

'My lords, we are required to raise one hundred and fifty thousand marks in order to secure the release of my son, the King of England, who as you know is currently held captive by Henry of Germany, the Holy Roman Emperor. I have ordered that the crypt of St Paul's Cathedral be converted into a vault in which the money will be stored, and each item will be deposited under either my seal or that of Walter de Coutances, Archbishop of Rouen and Chief Justiciar, who will also act as the collector of all revenues raised from our estates across the Channel. I look to you for suggestions as to how the money shall be raised.'

It fell briefly silent until William Marshall suggested, 'The Church must be made to contribute more than it has on occasions in the past. Priests, abbots, abbesses and even mendicant friars grow fat on the revenues enjoyed by their holy houses, while pleading the vow of poverty. Let them give more than their customary miserable tithe.'

'We shall need the support of the Church in making our plea to his Holiness for his intervention with the Holy Roman Emperor,' Hubert Walter objected.

'Her Majesty has already sought such intervention, and the response thus far has been silence,' de Coutances hastily advised the council. 'Although in holy orders myself, I cannot deny that the Church, both here and in our overseas domains, has grown wealthy during the years of peace that have blessed this land in recent times, thanks to the pious benevolence of King Richard.'

'A king who has barely been present within these shores since his coronation,' Henry FitzAilwin sneered. 'We can thank Prince John for his governance of the land in the king's lengthy absence, and now no doubt the merchants who I represent are to be fleeced in order to have King Richard released from a bondage that he exposed himself to in the first place.'

Nervous eyes drifted towards Queen Eleanor, expecting a bitter rebuke, but it was as if most of the fight had gone out of her. She smiled coldly at FitzAilwin and replied, 'We are all well aware of the way in which Prince John bribed your merchant citizens with a free charter, Master FitzAilwin. If you wish it to be confirmed by King Richard upon his return to England, then you would be as well to walk among your wealthier citizens with a large hat into which they may tip their gold.'

This evoked a few titters, and FitzAilwin bowed his reddened face in silent deference as Eleanor regained the initiative.

'I propose not a tithe — a traditional tenth — but a quarter of last year's income, to be donated by every freeman, every knight, every merchant, and every holy house. The sum we are required to raise exceeds the annual receipts to the Treasury by a good amount, so even the donation of a quarter will not suffice. Hubert Walter here has undertaken to visit every holy house in the realm, along with men at arms, in order to empty crypts, cellars, chapter houses, libraries and chapels of every item of precious metal that can be found therein. If his Holiness chooses to excommunicate me, or even to place the nation under interdict, then so be it. He has thus far failed me in my efforts to secure my son's release, so why should I fear his further disregard?'

'Might I enquire to what extent Prince John will be assisting in this pursuit of ransom money?' William Marshall asked pointedly. 'I last saw him in Southampton, but had assumed that he remained a member of this Regency Council. Is there some reason why he is not present among us today? We men of warfare have a crude expression in respect of someone who is untrustworthy; it is that we would rather have him in the tent, pissing out, than outside it, pissing in.'

The ribald laughter was silenced by an icy glare from Eleanor.

'Have a care, Marshall. I do not quarrel with your crude analogy, but I take great exception to hearing my youngest son described as untrustworthy.'

Most eyes fell to the table in response to this, and it was uncertain how the business might proceed. But just at that moment, Adele gave a cry of delight from where she stood looking out at the stable yard. She then rushed from the chamber with a brusque, 'Excuse me for one moment, madam.'

The council were still debating whether or not a quarter might be too high a sum to demand, and would therefore be met with strong resistance, when Adele reappeared, towing Earl William of Repton by the hand. Eleanor smiled a welcome and waved him towards one of the vacant seats.

'Most of you will already know the Earl of Repton, one of our King's Justices, and a member of this council. He was for a while the Chief Justice, but graciously stood aside when I asked de Coutances to assume the duties of Chief Justiciar. He is no doubt about to explain his late arrival.'

William bowed his head in recognition of the gentle rebuke. 'My sincere apologies, but I was not sure if I was still a member of the council, given the tumultuous events of recent months. In addition, I have been fully engaged in an investigation into the abuse of office by the High Sheriff of Nottinghamshire, Derbyshire and the Royal Forests, a man named William de Wendenal. He has engaged in brutal actions in order to rid an area known as the Shire Wood of its honest farmers, labourers and craftsmen for no better reason than to clear the forests for hunting. He has, regrettably, done so on the authority of one who was once — and still may be — a member of this council.'

'We will discuss this later,' Eleanor intervened sharply. 'In the meantime, welcome back, Earl William, and let us return to the matter of how to raise the sum required for the release of the king.'

Adele could hardly contain herself until the meeting adjourned, and the members of council drifted slowly away about their other business. Heedless of the fact that Eleanor was still seated in the chamber, she threw her arms around William and all but smothered him in kisses.

'It has been so long!' she murmured. 'I had heard that you had put yourself at the mercy of Prince John!'

A polite cough reminded them that they were not alone, and that the royal mother was listening to every word. Adele backed away and begged the queen's pardon, but Eleanor merely chuckled.

'I well recall the joys of past reunions, so I do not seek to chide you for displaying a true wifely devotion. However, I must perforce ask for some discretion when you refer to my youngest son as if he were evil. He is selfish, foolish, easily led and unreliable — but not evil.'

'Where is he now, Your Highness?' William asked.

Eleanor shrugged. 'It is difficult to know these days, but we parted company in Southampton. He was rumoured to be aiming to cross the Channel, in breach of his promise to join me here in London, in order to seek an alliance with Philip of France, who is one of those who has King Richard closely guarded. The prison is said to be somewhere in Germany, but the Holy Roman Emperor seeks to curry favour with Philip. I believe Philip of France to be the key to Richard's release, so perhaps we might consider a possible exchange with Princess Alys, who we still hold secure in Rouen under the guardianship of your son Hugh.'

'What of Robert?' Adele asked of her husband.

'He remains on our estate, but has proved his courage and manhood in seeking out outlaws hiding in the Shire Wood who can attest to the villainous actions of Sheriff de Wendenal,' said William.

'You made mention of someone of high standing who had condoned his actions,' Eleanor reminded him. 'Given that the hunting lodge in the Shire Wood has long been a royal favourite, and given that this sheriff has responsibility for Nottingham Castle, were you referring to my son John?'

William hesitated for a moment, then nodded. 'Regrettably so, Your Highness. Or so the man himself implied when I first chided him regarding his cruelty. It has gone far beyond that since, and I can only conclude that he defies my authority as a King's Justice because he enjoys the protection of someone very highly placed at court. I do not feel that I am unjustly accusing your son, and it is a matter of considerable regret to me to have to voice my suspicions.'

'You do well to do so,' Eleanor reassured him, 'and I thank you for your courage and honesty. I wish to employ both in the more urgent matter of securing the ransom for the release of my other son.'

'Your Highness?' William asked.

Eleanor frowned. 'There is need to justify the levying of a heavy one-quarter tax on every free man in the realm, plus the removal and sale of valuables from our many churches and monasteries. I do so with a heavy heart, but I require you to draft the necessary ordinance under the royal prerogative. I believe that I have the authority to proceed in such a fashion?'

'You do indeed, Your Highness, since the nation is at peril, positioned as it is with its king in thrall to its enemies, and with the ever present threat of invasion.'

'Good. It is as I thought. Please regard the drafting of the necessary ordinance as your highest priority. This means that your quarrel with a Nottingham sheriff must await its turn.'

When William's face expressed his disappointment, Eleanor made a clucking noise.

'The sooner you give me the authority to rescue one son from a foreign dungeon, the sooner you may set about proving the misdeeds of another. So lose no time in carrying out my orders.'

XX

William had just cause to be suspicious of Prince John's pretended loyalty to his older brother. No sooner had John parted from his mother, with the usual bare-faced assurance that he would support the family cause, than he had slipped behind the walls of Wallingford Castle, for many years a secure royal stronghold, and begun plotting. He had not the slightest intention of recognising the authority of the Regency Council, but he eagerly sought news of its decisions and policies from anyone he could bribe or threaten.

When he learned of Eleanor's strenuous efforts to raise the ransom money for Richard's release, John hit upon a plan to add to his own personal wealth while delaying, if not actually preventing, his brother's return to England. He had a copy of the royal seal created by a skilful forger, and sent his men to the more remote areas such as the West Country and the Scottish Borders, exacting wealth with the falsified authority of Eleanor's Ordinance. The considerable sum thus acquired went into his war chest in the vaults of Wallingford, some of which he used to buy more weaponry for his already substantial force of mercenaries, and the rest of which he employed in buying the loyalty of lesser barons with ambitions far beyond their means.

He also sent envoys to Philip of France with proposals designed to encourage him to venture further north into Normandy. Chief among these was an offer to rescue the reputation of the Princess Alys, now into her early thirties and suffering from severe depression arising from both Richard's rejection of her and her continued imprisonment. His offer was to marry her himself, with the intention that she would one day become the Queen of England, even though this would require him to divorce his existing wife, Isabella of Gloucester. It had been a marriage in name only after the first few months, following which her novelty had diminished for John. He had since resumed his acquisition of mistresses and siring of bastards. All that would be required would be valid grounds other than John's adultery, and their consanguinity as second cousins seemed a likely way to proceed.

John required only that Philip advance with his army through Normandy and lay siege to Rouen in order to secure the release of his sister, while negotiating for Richard's transfer from a German prison to a French one, where his death might be attributed to natural causes. However, this latter scheme met with stern resistance from Henry of Germany, who had already, along with Leopold of Austria, paid the price of excommunication by the Pope for his breach of the 'Truce of God'. For one thing, Henry did not wish such a powerful potential enemy to possess such a valuable bargaining counter, and for another he had become quite fond of his royal prisoner.

Richard had engaged his customary charm in making himself agreeable to his captors, and was soon being invited to partake at banquets, join in hunting parties, share crude jokes with soldiers who were nominally guarding him and display his musical talents. The restrictions on his freedom were eased by a bemused emperor to the extent that he was allowed to both send and receive messages, and in due course visitors. De Coutances was the chosen envoy, and through him Richard learned of the tireless efforts being made on his behalf to raise the ransom money; he was also able to send back messages of love and thanks to Eleanor. He laughed off warnings regarding

John's intrigues with a dismissive observation: 'My brother John is not the man to conquer a country if there is anyone to offer the feeblest resistance.'

In due course Henry of Germany was persuaded to amend the ransom terms. The sum to be handed over in the form of coinage was reduced to one hundred thousand marks, if an agreed number of sons of noble houses were also handed over as hostages for the remaining fifty thousand after Richard's release. A further sign that England and the Holy Roman Empire might soon become close allies was the proposed betrothal treaty between Frederick, the son of Leopold of Austria who was also Henry of Germany's nephew, with Eleanor of Brittany, Richard's niece and the sister of Richard's declared heir, Duke Arthur.

The growing friendship between Richard and Emperor Henry, and the revised terms for Richard's release, caused consternation in at least two nations. For England, although the reduction in the sum was a matter for rejoicing, there remained the agonising choice of the 'noble sons' who were to be handed over as surety. The members of council were called upon to set the example, although few of them had sons who were not already established in their own estates as mature adults. All eyes turned to William, who bowed his head and agreed to send Robert as one of the hostages from England.

Robert's reaction was a mixture of outrage, perceived betrayal and flat refusal. 'For one thing, you need me here to manage the estate,' he protested, 'and for another, I am your trusted contact with the men of the Shire Wood, who will eventually be your witnesses against Sheriff de Wendenal. Thirdly, I am shortly to be wed to Beth.'

'Not without my permission you're not,' William warned him, 'and as for your other arguments I can, I am sure, safely enter the Shire Wood without you as my escort. Finally, the estate can be left to manage itself, under the general guidance of Thomas Derby. He knows how to supervise others and tell them what to do. You will leave with me for London within the week.'

Robert stormed off, and William opted to let him fume and fuss in private, although no doubt with comfort from the comely Beth. Meanwhile, he occupied his time in learning of the current state of Repton Manor and issuing instructions to Thomas Derby, its nominal steward. It was not until the evening prior to his planned departure that he realised that Robert was missing, and had in fact not been seen around the estate for several days. William had no option but to return to Westminster, red-faced, and with the embarrassing tidings that his son had fled rather than answer England's call.

Richard's impending release had also caused consternation in Paris, to which John had fled when he'd heard that his treachery in diverting funds intended for Richard's release had been revealed to his mother. King Philip had sought in vain to persuade his rival Henry of Germany to increase the ransom demanded, or at least find some excuse to justify a delay in the release date. Henry had blankly refused all such requests, and Philip and John began considering the best tactics to adopt both before and after the anticipated release of their common enemy.

It was John's belief that if he could seize the English lands on that side of the Channel, he would be in a strong position to wage war on England and its newly restored King Richard, preferably before Richard was actually freed. He offered Philip some of the territories he hoped to capture in exchange for French men at arms to reinforce his somewhat threadbare force, and Philip agreed. Encouraged, John then contacted those barons in England who had declared their loyalty to his cause in the expectation of new estates and ordered them to rebel against the Regency Council. Enough of them were shallow and greedy enough to reveal John's plans in exchange for a pardon and territorial reward, and Eleanor immediately ordered the confiscation of all John's estates. She also revealed his treachery to Pope Celestine, who responded by excommunicating both John and Philip. In a wild rage, John headed north towards Rouen, intent on imprisoning Richard's new queen, Berengaria, as well as securing the release of his intended bride Alys.

Back in London, the council were increasingly confident as the ransom fund grew rapidly from the sale of confiscated estates following John's treacherous departure across the Channel. They had also learned of his villainy in collecting money intended to secure Richard's release and devoting it instead to the funding of his own army, and they had hauled several leading nobles before them to show why their estates should not be forfeit for their alliance with John, who had effectively abandoned them to their fate.

On William's advice, instead of having them put to death as traitors, they were forced to their knees and made to swear a new oath of allegiance to King Richard, in addition to surrendering their estates, which were then sold to eager purchasers. A triumphant Walter de Coutances announced to a gleeful council late in 1193 that they could finally cross the Channel in a heavily armed convoy, headed by the doughty and fearless William Marshall, with the now elderly Queen Eleanor borne in a litter in its centre. This time, there was a second litter bearing her faithful and almost lifelong companion and friend, Adele.

Deprived yet again of her company, and left behind as part of the remaining council that was to govern England in the interim, William turned his thoughts to Sheriff de Wendenal. He had more than enough evidence available to have the man arrested and charged with a series of atrocious crimes committed against the simple country folk that he was charged with the duty of protecting. William well recalled their first encounter, when he had made it abundantly clear that he was being protected — indeed encouraged — by Prince John. Although John had now fled the country, the council needed to be made aware of the full extent of his treachery, and in particular King Richard and his mother Eleanor would need a great deal of convincing before they held the errant brother and son fully to account.

He therefore rode back to his Repton estate, his hopes high that in his absence Robert might have returned, particularly since the noble sons had already been chosen and were part of Queen Eleanor's entourage as they rode south to Germany to secure Richard's release. But a sad-faced Thomas Derby shook his head when William made enquiry.

'We ain't seen 'im since 'e took off wiv Beth that time. God alone knows where 'e's got to, although 'e keeps in touch through me eldest, Peter, if yer remembers 'im. Peter an' 'is missus 'as a cottage down near the river, an' seemingly Robert calls on 'em late at night, mainly ter let us all know that 'e's still alive. But other than that, we knows nothin', I'm afraid.'

Swallowing his disappointment, William made arrangements for the lodging of the four men at arms he'd brought with him from London in order to assist in the arrest of de Wendenal.

Three days after his return, he and his entourage rode at daybreak through the entrance gates to the Repton estate. By the middle of the day, they were seated outside Nottingham

Castle, whose two heavy wooden gates were firmly shut against them, with armed men stationed both in front and on top of it. The fortress was clearly designed to withstand a siege, and intelligent use had been made of its position on a two-hundred-feet-high sandstone outcrop that was assailable at ground level only from the north.

William shouted up that he was a Royal Justice sent by the king, and that he had business with Sheriff de Wendenal, who was believed to be within. There was a lengthy delay while a message was sent back up to the castle, at the end of which the heavy oak gates creaked open and William and his men nudged their mounts through. They still had two more levels to climb, and their horses bent their heads forward as they patiently bore them up through the middle bailey. To one side there were archery butts at which the castle guard were no doubt ordered to practise regularly. They then passed through another set of gates that lay open at the centre of a curtain wall, and finally they had reached the upper bailey. The castle itself sat on a greensward that had recently been scythed, to judge by the smell of newly cut grass that threatened to make them sneeze.

They were met at the entrance by a man who introduced himself as the castellan. William was just asking himself why the sheriff did not exercise this function when several men at arms appeared behind them and offered to show William's men where they could refresh themselves after their journey. William gave them leave to do so, then followed the castellan down the stone-flagged hallway into the main hall. There de Wendenal sat at a long oak table, drinking wine with two older looking men who were heavily armed, and wearing a livery that William didn't recognise. De Wendenal looked up hopefully as he asked, 'You come from the king?'

'From those appointed to govern the nation in his absence, certainly,' William replied as he reached inside his tunic and removed a sheet of vellum. 'You may be aware that King Richard is currently held captive in Germany.'

'Indeed, God be praised,' de Wendenal sneered. 'Long may he remain in irons. But I was referring to the lawful monarch of England, King John.'

'*Prince* John was last heard of scuttling away to his ally King Philip of France like a rat departing from a sinking vessel,' William retorted. 'My authority comes from the Council of State assembled and authorised by Queen Dowager Eleanor. I have here the warrant for your arrest, countersigned by Chief Justiciar Walter de Coutances, prior to his departure in order to secure the release of the rightful King Richard.'

De Wendenal's sneer did not waver. 'They have finally raised the ransom money?'

'They have indeed. It is time for all those such as yourself, who have abused and betrayed the people under the pretended rule of Prince John, to pay the penalties for their crimes. In your case, it will no doubt be a hanging.'

De Wendenal put down his wine mug and laughed as he looked across the table at his henchmen. 'Brave words, for someone who stands alone in the presence of two of the best swordsmen in the county, inside one of its strongest fortresses, and armed only with a piece of parchment.'

'I have the law behind me,' William insisted, but less sure of his ground.

'The only thing behind you, you arrogant simpleton, are four armed men who will convey you to the dungeons below here. You appear to be well fed — if not best described as "portly", given your advanced years — but we shall see how long your frame can withstand the absence of food or drink. No-one will know what has become of you, and do not think to shout out for rescue. For one thing, the caves into which my dungeons are set are well beyond the hearing of all but a few peasants, whose cottages are in the lane below. Secondly, you will only weaken your constitution by such exercise without sustenance, and — perhaps more to the point — the men who accompanied you have already been hung from the castle walls, on my instruction.'

William turned in horror. As the sheriff had boasted, there were four rough-looking men at arms in the doorway, each with a hand on his sword hilt. Cursing himself for an arrogant fool, William allowed himself to be pushed, kicked, and dragged outside, through a metal grille set into the curtain wall, then down through a series of sandy corridors lit by rushlights. They reached a metal door that was pushed open with an ominous noise as it ground along the sandstone floor. One of the men held up a torch as two others hurled William bodily into the small chamber in which he was to be confined.

He barely had time to take in his surroundings before the torch light was removed and the door was slammed shut, but he was almost certain that in the far corner he had caught sight of a rotting skeleton in mouldering rags.

XXI

'Will my husband join me here in Rouen once he is freed?' Berengaria asked as she jealously watched Edwina breastfeeding baby Geoffrey.

Hugh looked on proudly before turning to Berengaria. 'The messenger from London did not say where Richard will be bound once he is released, but no doubt he will wish to lose little time before being reunited with you,' he replied. 'However, it is also rumoured that Prince John may be headed this way, in order to free Princess Alys.'

Berengaria sighed. 'My heart breaks for that poor woman, imprisoned here all these years after being promised the crown of England. But her loss is my gain, since one day I will sit on the throne that was once destined to be hers. However, I cannot but think how I would feel, were I in her position.'

'You must therefore pray that she is one day released,' Hugh said cautiously, 'but I hope that you will do nothing to assist in that, since both John of England and Philip of France would no doubt dearly wish to secure your person, to be held for ransom. I am in truth guarding *both* of you.'

'Is there any further news of John?' Edwina asked nervously.

Hugh shook his head. 'I know only that he landed at Calais some weeks ago, and could by now be in Paris. If he had intended to first lay siege to us here at Rouen, we would no doubt have seen his battle banners by now.'

Hugh was correct in his belief that John had been in Paris for some weeks. He was now pledged to marry Alys of France, to whose half-brother Philip he had sworn fealty for any English territories he might capture, in return for which Philip had made available a further thousand French men at arms. This all but doubled John's force, but he hesitated to ask for more. For one thing, time was of the essence if he was to strike before the rumoured impending release of Richard. Secondly, it was unlikely that any of the Normandy fortresses that he planned to attack on his way north to Rouen would have sufficient men to resist even such a reduced number.

The first to yield were Gisors and Évreux, their commanders preferring to hand over their castles rather than have all their men slaughtered. Considerably heartened, John pushed on towards Rouen, his northern scouts advising him of a heavily protected caravan of men at arms and wagons passing through Amiens and Reims. It was on its way south-east towards the German border and Speyer, where the exchange of prisoners and ransom money was to take place.

Lookouts and scouts to the south of Rouen Palace soon brought news to Hugh that they had sighted a large body of armed men riding in their direction. He quickly put into action the plan that he had been devising for some weeks for the protection of the three important women for whose lives he was responsible. The royal Palace of Rouen was built for comfort rather than defence, and it more closely resembled the nearby cathedral in its architecture. Hugh was apprehensive of his ability to hold it against a large army, even given his unusually large garrison of five hundred men. Were it to fall, then not only would John be able to release Princess Alys — who, it was rumoured, he planned to marry — but he would also no doubt take Berengaria as a hostage against whatever plans Richard had to punish his younger brother for his rebellion. And wherever Berengaria went, no doubt Edwina would insist on accompanying her, such was their closeness. And with Edwina would go their defenceless son Geoffrey.

None of this could be contemplated for a moment, and it was time to take urgent action.

Against the strident protests of the women, Hugh ordered them down into the crypt of the cathedral, with fifty men at arms guarding its entrance doors and sworn to protect the lives of the ladies with their own. Then he organised the remaining men in the palace into squares of twelve, closely resembling the old Roman battle formations. They were located in front of each principal doorway leading into the palace, and sworn not to yield until the last one of them fell to an enemy sword. Then Hugh took up his own position, in the centre of the main courtyard, sitting astride his horse as he gave orders for the main gates to be opened.

He did not have long to wait. The distant clatter of horses' shod hooves on stone cobbles drifted into the courtyard on the gentle westerly breeze, and before long the first line of enemy cavalry rode in, their battle surcoats emblazoned with the lions of England. They wheeled into a semi-circle that was left open at its top, and through the gap marched five ranks of foot soldiers, four abreast, with the fleur-de-lys emblems on their shields leaving no-one in any doubt that John had secured the armed support of Philip of France. A herald somewhere sounded a regal blast, and into the courtyard rode the man who had been plotting for most of his life to become King of England.

John reined in his horse and looked contemptuously down at Hugh. 'Your face is familiar to me. I do not know where we last met, but I suspect that it must have been in a madhouse, if you seek to defend this pisspot of a palace against the might of both England and France.'

'As for my supposed insanity,' Hugh yelled back up at him, 'I am not opposing the might of England and France. I am opposing merely a single traitor who would usurp the crown of England from his own brother — the man with a more lawful claim to it, and the man whose bravery was there for all to see when I accompanied him on his journey to the Holy Land. I have yet to hear of any qualities in you that would persuade me to follow in your cause.'

'If you would simply yield up the Princess Alys and the pretended Queen Berengaria, I shall depart without bloodshed,' John called down, 'and you may regard yourself as the *seigneur* of Rouen. If you choose to resist, you will expire dismally in your own welter, a martyr to your own stupidity.'

'My uncle was martyred on the orders of your father,' Hugh yelled back. 'He served Archbishop Becket at Canterbury, and died in a vain attempt to preserve that man of God from your father's butchers. So you see, insanity runs in my family.'

'So shall your blood, you arrogant cretin!' John yelled, then turned angrily in the saddle. '*What?*' he demanded of the lone horseman who had clattered into the courtyard during the last exchange and tugged urgently at John's chainmail sleeve.

The response was intended as a hoarse whisper, but the stone surroundings of the courtyard amplified his words enough for Hugh to catch them. 'A message from my master King Philip of France, my lord. Richard of England has been released from bondage, it would seem, and is riding back to claim his throne. My master's message is: "Look to yourself — the Devil is loosed"!'

To Hugh's profound relief, John gave a startled yell and turned his horse's head sharply before digging in the spurs. The horse whinnied and reared, then bolted out of the courtyard, leaving John's bemused entourage to follow him out into the street. The mocking curses of Hugh's men pursued them as they departed.

XXII

Three days later, as Hugh was eating supper in his private chambers with Edwina, a page came urgently through the door without knocking.

'Sir,' he blurted out, 'there are more armed men in the courtyard, asking for you.'

Hugh hastily donned his battle mail, strapped his sword belt to his midriff and took the steps down two at a time. He only came to a halt with sighs of relief when he recognised the imposing figure of William Marshall, standing with his horse's bridle in his hand.

'Bad news?' Hugh asked.

Marshall shrugged. 'It depends upon your priorities, I suppose. The good news for the nation is that King Richard is free, and will cross the Channel back to England as soon as I rejoin the royal party. I have made this brief diversion at the request of Queen Eleanor, who has received tidings that your father has been imprisoned within Nottingham Castle. Its sheriff is demanding safe passage out of England in return for his release without harm.'

'I must lose no time in seeking to rescue him!' Hugh proclaimed, then his face fell as the reality of his position sunk in. 'But I cannot leave my post here, guarding the new queen, and ensuring that Princess Alys is not freed by her brother or Prince John. But surely King Richard wishes Berengaria to be escorted to him for their reunion — is that not why you are here?'

Marshall smiled knowingly. 'I have no such instruction — in fact, no instruction at all. Richard is attended by Queen

Eleanor, who is of course attended by your mother, the Countess of Repton. In the circumstances, I believe that I can justify leaving some of my men here under the command of one of my captains, while you make such haste as you are able to secure your father's release from confinement. Will you first journey back with me to be reunited with King Richard?'

'No,' Hugh replied firmly. 'No doubt His Majesty has other matters that he will regard as more urgent and important, such as his journey across the Channel and his resumption of authority. There are also some rebel castles, of which Nottingham is one. When I last heard, they were holding out for Prince John. I shall make haste to take ship from Le Havre, and from there make landfall on the south coast of England. I can be back on the family estate of Repton with three or four days of hard riding, and once there I am but a further two hours' ride from Nottingham. Tell King Richard that I shall assess its fitness to be placed under siege, and I thank you most sincerely for your generous offer to accept responsibility for the defence of Rouen.'

'Think nothing of it,' Marshall said. 'It is but a small favour in return for your bravery in the Mediterranean, without which Richard would have lost his mother, his sister and his bride. God speed in your efforts.'

Edwina screamed in protest when Hugh told her that he was leaving immediately to negotiate for the release of his father.

'Why may I not come with you?' she demanded, hands on hips.

He took her in his arms and held her tightly. 'With our infant son under your arm? Or did you propose to abandon him here? And if it comes to that, you are bound in service to Queen Berengaria, and will no doubt be required to be by her side when she travels to her coronation.'

'Has King Richard called for her?'

'Not yet, but that moment cannot be long delayed. In the meantime, I shall be obliged to ride at a speed that no woman with a child in her arms could possibly maintain. Believe me when I say that it grieves me for us to be parted again, but I cannot sit idly by while my father languishes in some pestilential prison cell. He is not a robust man of warfare like me, but a somewhat elderly and portly lawyer to whom hardship and deprivation could prove fatal. You must surely see why I must lose no time in returning to England?'

Edwina grudgingly nodded, but insisted that Hugh say a long farewell to their son Geoffrey. As he held him tightly to his chest, Hugh whispered, 'Perhaps one day you will be required to rescue *your* father from some threatened evil. If so, I hope you can also harden your heart against the sorrow of parting from loved ones.'

He turned away with tears forming in his eyes, and Edwina held him to her one final time as she sobbed her farewells, then ran from the chamber. Hugh handed Geoffrey back to his nurse and headed swiftly downstairs to the stables before he lost his nerve.

Less than a week later, the royal barque, the *Trenchemer*, summoned across the Channel by a king's envoy, took on board the most precious cargo it had ever carried — the King of England. Richard arrived in Sandwich on the morning of 12th March, 1194. It was the first time that his feet had touched English soil in over three years. On his mother's insistence, they lost no time in riding to Canterbury, to give thanks for his safe return at the shrine of Saint Thomas Becket.

Adele, Countess of Repton, had prayers of her own to offer as she obtained permission from her mistress to spend an entire night on her knees inside the sanctuary, praying for the safe delivery of her ageing husband. Eleanor had broken the news to her once they were back in England, but had insisted that she should remain with the royal party, rather than hasten north to join their son. William Marshall had assured her that Hugh was more than capable of establishing the true position, and would only be distracted from his task if also called upon to console a grieving mother.

While at Canterbury, Richard received some disturbing news from its archbishop, Hubert Walter. He had recently dined with a cleric sent over by John from his base in Paris, who, overawed by the honour being paid to him as a guest of the Primate of All England — and perhaps under the influence of the fine wine — revealed that he had been sent on a mission to instruct all those loyal to John to defend their castles against the returning Richard. The man was subsequently arrested, and the papers he was carrying were read to the council members who were part of the triumphant returning party. The unanimous advice given to Richard was that he should strike quickly and hard against the rebels thereby identified, who had not received the command from John.

Rather than delay his re-entry to London, Richard allocated the mission to suppress the rebel castles to those members of council in a position to do so. Within days, he had received the formal surrender of Tickhill, Marlborough and Lancaster.

The triumphant progress through the streets of London came next. Richard and his men rode sedately through strings of gaily decorated banners towards St Paul's Cathedral, where further prayers of thanks were offered to its patron saint. From St Paul's they progressed along the Strand to Westminster Palace, with cheering crowds giving thanks to God for Richard's return.

Any further celebrations were put on hold as those sent to assess the state of the nation returned with their reports. The only castle still in rebel hands was the one in Nottingham. The Earls of Huntingdon, Chester and Ferrers reported gloomily that not only was it all but impregnable — standing atop a two-hundred-foot cliff and accessible at ground level only from the north — but its guardian, the sheriff of the three counties by which it was surrounded, refused to believe that King Richard had returned, and had challenged the royal emissaries to do their worst.

'And by God I shall!' Richard thundered as he thumped the supper table. 'Not only does he support a weak usurper who was unfortunate enough to be born in my shadow, not only does he defy my order to surrender, but he has laid hands on a valued officer of the Crown, whose son was the saviour of those dear to me on our journey to Outremer. Who is this upstart dog who claims to answer only to my brother John?'

'Sheriff de Wendenal, sire,' Earl Ferrers told him. 'There are many stories told of his cruelty to those abiding in the lands surrounding Nottingham. It was well known that the Royal Justice, the Earl of Repton, who is now confined in his dungeons, was seeking to hold him to account for his misdeeds.'

'What the Earl of Repton has begun, we shall complete!' Richard yelled. 'Summon your forces to regather here at Westminster two days hence. We ride in force to Nottingham!'

Hugh sat before the dying fire in the hall of Repton Manor, idly wondering whether or not to go outside for more logs. He doubted he would be able to sleep, despite his exhaustion after so many days in the saddle, interrupted only by a lumpy five-hour crossing of the Channel to Portsmouth in a wine cargo barque.

Hugh's mind rotated the options again. The first, and most natural to him, was to storm the castle with an armed force of his own, but from what he'd been advised about its position, that seemed impractical, even had he possessed the men. A second possibility was to seek an audience with the man holding his father captive — allegedly the local sheriff, who was in the pay of Prince John — and claim to be acting in King Richard's name as he demanded the release of his father and the surrender of the castle. Even assuming that he was believed, a single armed man on a horse would hardly seem like a genuine emissary of a powerful king. And, of course, he might well finish up chained alongside his father.

He had just come back to the third option — the most practical of all, but the weakest — when the door opened, letting in a sharp blast of the late spring gale. A man stood in the shade of the doorway, wrapped in a cloak that more closely resembled an animal skin.

Hugh broke the silence. 'Do I know you?' he demanded.

The man grinned. 'You should, since we're brothers.'

Hugh remembered, and smiled back. 'Sorry, Robert, but they told me you'd run away.'

'Did they also tell you that I come back occasionally at night, to see Peter and his wife? And is it true that Father's being held captive by de Wendenal?'

'If he's the local sheriff, then that's correct.'

'Where I've been hiding they don't like de Wendenal, so if you're going to take an army up there to slit his throat, we'd like to watch.'

'And to whom are you referring when you say "we"?'

'Some friends of mine who I live with now, along with Beth. We're married, by the way.'

'That doesn't surprise me,' Hugh said, 'since she's a comely lass. Did you seek Father's permission?'

'He said he wouldn't give it unless I agreed to become a hostage somewhere across the Channel. But there's a friendly holy brother where I live, and he insisted when we found out that Beth's expecting. The baby's due in the summer.'

'Congratulations. I now have a son of my own that I had to leave behind in Rouen when I came home to secure Father's release.'

'And have you any idea how you might do that?'

'No, to be perfectly honest with you. All I can think of at this stage is to ask what terms the sheriff's demanding for his safe return.'

'How do you know he's still alive?' Robert asked. 'Sheriff de Wendenal is as tricky as one of the ferrets that my friend Much puts down rabbit warrens to win us our supper.'

'So you think I should demand to see Father before I begin negotiating for his release?'

'Not you,' Robert suggested. 'Somebody else — like me, for instance. If you go in there on your own, what's to stop him locking you away as well? Then, if you're regarded as sufficiently important to King Richard — or whoever rules the country at present other than Prince John — the sheriff's got *two* hostages to bargain with, hasn't he?'

'So you're proposing to come with me and go inside the castle to satisfy yourself that Father's still alive?'

'Not on my own, no. I may be just a simple estate manager, but once de Wendenal finds out whose son I am, then I'll be as vulnerable as you are to being locked away. I'll take some friends with me, from where I live now.'

'And where *is* that, exactly?'

'You don't need to know. Just be here tomorrow, around the middle of the day.'

With no other viable option, the following day Hugh did as Robert had requested. Just as he rose from his modest dinner, Robert re-entered the hall along with three rough-looking farm labourers, who he introduced with obvious pride.

'This is Alan, this one's Hugh, and the big man's John. We're all set to go, if you are. Can we borrow the wagon, to save us having to walk any further? Only we've been on the road since daybreak.'

The afternoon shadows were beginning to lengthen as they stood in front of the intimidating oak gates that seemed to be the main entrance to the castle. Hugh called out to the gate guards that he wished to speak to Sheriff de Wendenal.

'What makes yer think 'e'll wanna talk ter *you*?' one of the guards demanded.

'It's in connection with the prisoner he's holding, who's our father,' Hugh replied.

The guard looked back at him disbelievingly. 'What, *all* of yer? Even that big bloke?'

'No, just me and him,' Hugh replied as he pointed to Robert. 'Now, do we get to speak to your master or not?'

The man disappeared by way of a flap cut into the big heavy doors, and Hugh, Robert and the others lowered their weary bones onto the bed of the cart that had carried them from Repton while they awaited a response. Eventually there came a bellow from the platform above the gate, and Hugh looked up for his first sight of Sheriff de Wendenal.

'I thought someone of importance was here,' the sheriff complained. 'Am I expected to negotiate terms with a bunch of smelly peasants?'

'I am Hugh of Repton,' Hugh shouted back up, 'the son of the Earl of Repton, who you have inside your dungeon. This man by my side is my younger brother, and we are here to enquire what might be your terms for our father's release.'

'I have already made those known to someone much closer to the centre of power than you, young man,' de Wendenal sneered.

'I am aware of that,' Hugh replied haughtily, 'since William Marshall, Earl of Pembroke, advised me that you are seeking a pardon for your treasonous acts, and safe passage out of England.'

'You have been in France, presumably?' de Wendenal asked.

'I was, but by now the king should be back in England, and seeking out those who proved false in his absence.'

'Well, you are aware of my terms,' de Wendenal said dismissively as he turned to leave. 'Come back with King Richard and we might then speak again.'

'How can we be sure that Father's still alive?' Robert yelled after him.

De Wendenal turned and smirked. 'You can't, can you?'

'Then neither can anyone,' Hugh reminded him. 'If King Richard comes here, as come here he will in due course, then who will reassure him that you have something to bargain with?'

De Wendenal thought briefly, then yelled down, 'Supposing I let you see him for long enough to satisfy yourself that he remains alive?'

'Not me,' Hugh replied as Robert kicked his ankle, 'my brother here.'

'Along with two of my friends,' Robert added.

'You do not trust me?'

'No, to be perfectly honest with you,' said Robert. 'So prove me wrong.'

Another moment's silence was followed by instructions to the guard to allow the three men through the small door set into the gate. Robert, along with Alan of the Dale and Hugh Meathanger, slipped through it, then wound their way, under escort, up to the castle before disappearing from Hugh's line of sight. Hugh climbed back onto the bed of the cart and looked inquisitively at the giant of a man they called John.

'I wonder why Robert didn't choose you to ensure his safety,' he mused.

John grinned. 'I've bin known ter frighten folk wiv me size, an' mebbe the sheriff wouldn't've agreed ter me goin' in. Robert's not stupid, in case yer wond'rin'.'

'How tall *are* you, exactly?' Hugh asked.

'Seven foot, bar an inch. But the inch don't matter when the bloke yer fightin's only five foot four.'

That was effectively the end of the conversation until Robert and his two companions reappeared through the castle gate flap. A broad grin was evident on Robert's face even from a distance. He walked over to where John was leaning on the wagon and nodded down the track towards the River Leen that ran almost under the walls, with a few buildings seemingly built into the rock on which the castle stood.

'Can you see that building along the river bank that has the flag on its roof, John?'

'Yeah, why?'

'You're needed down there without delay. We have a job for your long arms. Go quickly.'

John set off at a brisk pace, and Hugh turned to Robert.

'You were looking very pleased with yourself when you left the castle — what have you been up to?'

'Freeing Father from his cell. He's still alive, but very weak, and we need to get him down the chute that leads into that building I just sent John to. It's the castle brewhouse, and there's a shaft that leads up through the caves into the castle itself.'

'How did you know that?'

'I didn't when we went in, but we found it when we headed downhill after getting Father out of his cell and carrying him down. We came to this room that had a winch in it, leading down through a shaft. I lowered Alan onto it and he found the brewhouse underneath. We fastened Father to the rope, and now we need John to reach up and pull him down through the hole into the brewhouse. When he's done that, we can carry Father out of there and get a physician to attend him.'

'How did you get him out in the first place?' Hugh asked, awestruck by their change of fortune.

'My good friend Hugh Meathanger here used to be a butcher before his trade was taken from him by the sheriff's men. He therefore has a talent with sharp knives, and can engage them very swiftly. The sheriff was unwise enough to send only two jailors down with us when we went to see Father's cell. Once the door had been opened, Alan and I held one each while Hugh opened their throats. Then we dressed one of the dead bodies in Father's rags and left him on the floor of the cell, facing the other way, so that anyone looking through the spying hole will think that Father's still in there.'

'What did you do with the other body?'

'It's in the room with the winch, where we left it. We were thinking of sending it down into the brewhouse, but decided that we'd been gone long enough, so went back up the way we'd come.'

'Didn't anyone enquire after the guards who'd gone down with you?'

'No, but if they had we were going to say that they were still down there, replenishing the rushlights. Here comes John — let's take the wagon down the track and collect Father, shall we?'

Hugh had to suppress a scream of horror when he saw the state of their father, naked, emaciated and stinking, with sores all over his lips and eyes. They poured ale into his mouth in the hope of enabling him to speak, then left off when he began to choke because he couldn't swallow. So they loaded him onto the cart and led the bullock back into town until they found a backstreet house whose crudely printed lintel sign announced the presence of a physician. Slipping the man ten marks, they urged him to do what he could, then carefully carried William up the rickety stairs.

In the far distance, they heard a horn being blown. Hugh looked up sharply and instructed Robert to remain with their father while he went to investigate.

'It's a street entertainer, surely?' Robert suggested.

Hugh shook his head. 'If you'd spent as much time as I have in court, you'd recognise a herald's blast. If God has smiled on us once again, King Richard's entering the town, and now Sheriff de Wendenal has *really* got something to worry about.'

XXIII

Unsure whose army might be invading Nottingham, Hugh crept slowly back through the streets that led towards the castle. Long before he reached it, he began to overtake weary foot soldiers, some of whom he recognised, and some of whom called out to him in a cheery but respectful greeting. He quickened his pace and eventually found himself back on the ground between the castle and a row of houses that formed the first of the town dwellings. In the centre, surrounded by his personal guard, sat King Richard on a splendid black courser decked out in cloths decorated with the lions of England.

Richard looked down with a smile as he saw Hugh appear to the side of his mount's tossing head. 'I thought I might meet you here,' he called down, 'since William Marshall advised me that your father has been taken prisoner by the local sheriff.'

'He was, sire, but we rescued him. He's still alive, but barely so, and I have a score to settle, if I might be permitted to re-enlist. But I have no horse at present.'

Richard nodded towards the castle gates. 'Horses are not necessary in a siege. I shall issue the usual offer, then retire for the night if — or perhaps it is more likely to be *when* — that offer is rejected. Let us see, shall we?' He ordered his herald to sound a blast on his battle horn, then rose in his stirrups so his shout might carry for a greater distance. 'I am King Richard of England, and I demand the immediate surrender of this royal castle into my hands. I shall grant merciful pardons to those who choose to desert and join my force, but I shall deliver guaranteed death to those who do not. Please convey this message to whoever pretends to be in command here.'

There was a familiar whirring sound, as a crossbow bolt sailed a few feet to the left of Richard's head and thudded into the wooden wall of the house behind him.

'Let us hope that such is the mark of their accuracy with a crossbow,' he said to Hugh. 'Please join me for a mug of wine once we've found suitable lodging.'

The 'suitable lodging' proved to be that of one of the town's wealthiest merchants, located in Greyfriars. It was named after the monastery that ran for most of its length. Meat, bread, cheese and fruit were hastily produced for the royal guest as he sat with Hugh on one side and the Earl of Chester on the other.

Richard turned to Hugh. 'You have presumably seen the inside of the castle? What did you learn of its defences?'

'In truth, sire, I have never been inside it,' Hugh confessed.

The king raised his eyebrows. 'How, then, did you rescue your father?'

'That was the work of some friends of my brother — men condemned as outlaws by Sheriff de Wendenal, who had no love for him. They overpowered the guards on the pretext of ensuring that Father was still alive, then brought him down by way of a series of caves that house the dungeons, but also lead down to the castle brewhouse on the banks of the river that runs alongside it.'

'So the castle may be entered secretly from this brewhouse?' Richard asked eagerly.

Hugh shook his head. 'No, sire — not by armed men, anyway. It was necessary to lower my father down through a cleft in the rock that is served by a winch. This is used to convey beer up to the castle.'

Richard swallowed his disappointment. 'Your father remains alive? If so, then he must have seen the inside of the castle. Could he assist with information, think you?'

'Regrettably, sire, he is still at risk of death. He is very weak, lying in the nearby house of a local physician. But my brother attends him, and he was inside the castle grounds in order to secure Father's escape.'

'I would speak with your brother,' Richard insisted.

Hugh nodded with obvious reluctance. 'I will go and bring him hither, sire, but he is currently at our father's bedside.'

'Bring him to me,' Richard instructed, 'and tell the physician that he must do all in his power to restore your father to health. Advise him, if you have not already, that he is ministering to a Royal Justice highly regarded by the king, and that his reckoning may be presented to the Royal Almoner in Westminster.'

A few minutes later, Hugh climbed the rickety staircase to the upper room in the physician's house and joined Robert, who sat gazing down at their father's gaunt, ash-white countenance.

'How goes he?' Hugh asked anxiously.

Robert shrugged. 'He remains in life, but barely. He still cannot swallow, not even the potions that the physician is urging upon him, but occasionally his eyes will open, and there is a faint smile on his face.'

While he was speaking, William turned his head on the bolster, opened his eyes and spoke to them both in a cracked voice. 'I knew you would both amount to something one day. Tell the mountebank that I am ready for one of his potions, though it be the death of me.'

'God be praised!' Robert sighed as he rose to his feet, but Hugh put out a hand to restrain him.

'I can do that. The king wishes to see you, and he may be found in that big house to the side of the monastery of Grey Friars, several streets away. Lose no time.'

'Your mother?' William croaked as Robert disappeared down the stairs.

Hugh gripped his hand reassuringly. 'Safe in London, with Queen Eleanor, no doubt. Do you wish her summoned here?'

'I am not for death yet,' William grinned weakly. 'And no doubt Queen Eleanor will have other duties for her. But give her my love. Will I be taken back to Repton?'

'Once you have enough strength,' Hugh promised him. 'And for that you must take the potions that you seem to despise.'

'Have you ever tasted rats' entrails?'

'Not recently, no,' Hugh said.

'Then do not seek to criticise one who shrinks from doing so,' came the reply, and Hugh went down the stairs with a smile, thanking God that his father had regained his sense of humour.

Having been ushered into the royal presence, an awe-stricken Robert knelt respectfully in front of the supper table and bowed his head.

Richard smiled. 'You are the brother of Hugh of Repton?'

'So I am advised by our father, Your — Your…'

'The usual term of address is "Majesty",' Richard said with amusement, 'but "sire" is more convenient, and takes less time. Now, they tell me that you rescued your father along with some friends. Is that the case?'

'Yes, sire. Some worthy men from the Shire Wood, unjustly condemned as outlaws. I have been living amongst them for some weeks now.'

'Outlaw or no, what can you tell me of what lies beyond the outer wall of the castle?'

'What you can see for yourself, sire, since the ground slopes upwards all the way. Once through the main gates you pass through some outer grounds, then through a further set of gates, less sturdy than the first set, then into a middle ground where they practise archery, then through a final gap in a wall and you find yourself at the doors of the keep itself.'

'From what you say, once an army of men has breached those first gates, the going is suitable for armed knights on horseback?'

'Not only suitable, sire, but admirable. I saw nought of any horses while I was inside the grounds. Mind you, I was bound there on other business.'

'Business that had a most welcome outcome. Is it true that there exists some sort of entrance to the castle through a brewhouse by a river?'

'Not for armed men, sire. It is used only for the delivery of beer casks.'

'A pity, although perhaps one day another invader might make use of it to their advantage. You made mention of friends who have been living in nearby woodland — men proclaimed to be outlaws. Would they rally to my cause, think you?'

'With the greatest of joy, sire,' said Robert. 'They are expert bowmen, and very skilled with knives and staves.'

'And they brought your father down through this brewhouse entry to the castle?'

'Yes, sire.'

'So they could climb back up through it, could they not?'

'No doubt, sire, but you would need to ask them.'

'That I shall do, Robert. Can you have them here by daybreak?'

'If I might be allowed the use of one of your baggage wagons, sire. There are many of them.'

'The more the merrier. You may have such wagons as you require, and the Earl of Chester here will see to your requirements. Go with him, then return on the morrow with your friends skilled in activities that we might put to good use.'

Hugh was both surprised, and a little apprehensive, when he re-entered the square in front of the castle the following morning to discover that it more closely resembled a marketplace. There were dozens of men clad in rough garments, grimy-faced but seemingly pleased to be swilling pots of ale and munching on hunks of bread and cheese. Hugh recognised Robert in the middle of the group and walked across with a quizzical smile.

'This will shortly become a battlefield of sorts,' he told Robert, 'so if your friends have come to watch, then they would be well advised to stand back.'

Robert chuckled and nodded at John Nailer. 'Go and tell *him* to disperse, and see what reward you receive.'

'He's rather too large for me,' Hugh admitted as he gazed in awe at the seven-foot mountain dressed like some sort of monstrous sheep. 'But who *are* these people?'

'They are my friends from the Shire Wood, with whom I have been residing ever since Father tried to haul me off to France as a hostage. Come and meet their leader.'

Hugh was led into the centre of the group, where a man of approximately his own age was bending a longbow as if testing it for strength. He looked up with a grin as he saw Robert and Hugh approaching, then looked Hugh's chainmail up and down. 'You must be Robert's oft talked-of brother, who serves King Richard,' he said. 'I am Robert of Swinecote, but those who accompany me call me "Robin". We have been asked by King Richard to assist in the re-taking of this castle that Sheriff de Wendenal seems to think is his.'

They became aware that everyone around them had fallen to their knees. King Richard, dressed from head to foot in his full battle armour, and accompanied by the Earl of Chester, similarly attired, walked into the group and gave a hand gesture that summoned them all back to their feet.

'I assume that you are the men of the Shire Wood,' he said. 'Who is your leader, if you have one?'

'It is I, Your Majesty,' Robin told him as he stepped forward. 'My men are yours to command.'

'Are there, among you, those who recently brought the Earl of Repton out of yon castle by an unusual route?'

'That'd be me an' two others,' Little John replied as he stepped forward.

Richard stared in disbelief at the man's size. 'Do you think you could lead a group of men back up through that opening and into the castle?'

'Not dressed like that,' John replied gruffly as he nodded towards the king's battle armour. 'They'd get stuck like a duck's egg up a hen's arse.'

Richard waited for the responding merriment to subside before replying. 'I had more in mind a group dressed like yourself, my good man. Once inside the castle, I would require you to slit throats.'

'Per'aps as well,' John grinned back, ''cos once we're in there, there's lotsa throats we'd like ter slit.'

'Excellent!' Richard beamed back. 'In a few moments, we shall begin our attack on the outer gates. When we do so, take such men as you require and climb up the "hen's arse", as you call it, and create whatever havoc you can from the inside.'

John Nailer, Hugh Meathanger and Alan of the Dale slid away with throaty chuckles of anticipation.

Richard turned to Hugh. 'You remember those battering rams we used to good effect at Acre?'

'No, sire, but you may recall that I was never in Outremer, because you sent me back with the ladies.'

'Indeed, so perhaps you did not get to see the one I have named "John". I gave it that name because of its ability to cause havoc. It has been brought back to England and hauled up here for the purpose that you are about to witness.'

Richard gave a curt instruction, and from a side-street there was a rumbling, creaking noise that grew louder as the most enormous battering ram Hugh had ever laid eyes on was pulled into place by four shire horses. They were then unharnessed and replaced by a dozen men, each of whom picked up a rope attached to its front end and began to haul it towards the front gates of the castle before Richard commanded them to halt.

'I should perhaps give this rat de Wendenal one final opportunity to leave his sinking ship,' Richard announced as he climbed back onto his courser, rose in the stirrups and bellowed up at the castle walls. 'I wish to speak with your self-proclaimed leader, who was until this moment the High Sheriff of Nottinghamshire, Derbyshire and the Royal Forests. You have just been replaced in office by the man to my right, William de Ferrers, Earl of Derby, which means that you no longer have any right — even a pretended one — to refuse me entry to this royal castle. I now make one final demand that you yield it up.'

'I will do so only if I am guaranteed safe passage out of England,' a thin voice replied, and on the battlements atop the outer wall could be seen the helmeted face of de Wendenal.

Richard gave a hollow laugh. 'I will guarantee you only a fair trial for treason. Since fair trials do not appear to be something with which you are familiar, you may of course decline, but if you do so, then it is unlikely that you will come out of there alive.'

'In that case,' came the reply, 'do your worst!'

'Let it be recalled that I *did* try,' Richard grinned as he gave orders for the battering ram to be hauled into place, prior to the cogs at the rear being wound back before its release.

However, the design fault that had been obvious to Hugh when he first caught sight of 'John' became fatally apparent as the men attempting to haul it forward came under a hail of crossbow bolts from the platform above the main gate. Eight of them remained as corpses on the dusty ground as the other four beat a hasty retreat. Clearly no-one had thought it necessary to place a shield roof above the ram, to protect those who were hauling it.

This happened three more times before Robin stepped out of the crowd of onlookers and knelt before the king.

'You recall, sire, that you invited us to partake of the festivities? May we now engage in what we do best? If you would care to send in more men with that device, we can sweep the scum off the wall above.'

Richard gave the command, and as the defenders appeared on the wall with loaded crossbows, Robin gave another command, and a dozen of his men stepped forward and let fly with their longbows. The defenders could be heard screaming as another row appeared behind them, only to fall under another blizzard of arrows.

By this stage, the battering ram had been towed into place in front of the gates. Four men behind it began hauling on the ropes that brought a mighty trunk of solid oak slowly to the rear of the contraption on a series of cogs. When it was fully back, two other men ran forward armed with heavy wooden slabs that were slipped into place between the final two cogs, acting as a sort of brake. A final command rang out across the open space and the brake slabs were hammered out from between the cogs, allowing the heavy oak ram to career forward and smash into the wooden gates with a splintering sound.

A rousing cheer went up from the men of Richard's army as the process was repeated twice more. The gates sagged on their hinges before flying open and falling to the ground in several shattered lumps. Richard raised his hand high in the air, and fifty armed knights on horseback leapt through the gap and cantered up the slope to the second gate, which was hastily abandoned by its almost token guard force. Foot soldiers began racing up the driveway and finishing off all the scattering defenders they could locate, and by the time that the cavalry halted at the castle door, all resistance seemed to have ceased.

Richard and his immediate house guard rode sedately up the slope, and the king grinned with sadistic satisfaction as he saw the grounds littered with the dead and the dying. Then as he reined in his horse at the front door, three men came strolling out through it, one of them looking somewhat sheepish as he held up a human head. It was still dripping with warm blood that was creating a light mist in the cool air.

'I 'opes as 'ow yer don't mind, Yer 'Ighness,' Hugh Meathanger muttered, 'but I think this is the bloke yer was lookin' fer. I 'opes as 'ow yer didn't want 'im tekken alive. It's that bastard de Wendenal. When we come up from the dungeons, we come across 'im tryin' ter come down the other way. We chased 'im inter the buildin', an' Little John were all fer rippin' 'is 'ead clean off his shoulders. I decided ter slit 'is throat instead, only I got a bit carried away, an' 'is 'ead come clean off.'

Richard burst out laughing. 'You merely saved the nation the cost of a trial. That tall man alongside you might wish to take it down to the front gate and impale it on one of those spikes, so all know what to expect if they resist the royal authority. Then let us all repair to the town, where you good fellows can drink yourselves into a stupor at my expense.'

Hugh was halfway up the driveway on foot when he stood to one side to allow Little John to pass him with the grisly trophy. Then he bowed his head to the approaching Richard, calling out, 'Was that who I thought it was, sire?'

'It was indeed, Hugh. You are invited to dinner, and to the meeting of the council that I shall be convening here in due course. Your justification for being in attendance will be revealed to you before then, but once your father is back in Repton, see to it that there is venison in the kitchen.'

XXIV

Propped up against the bolster, William opened his eyes and smiled as he felt the soft hand in his and recognised the tear-streaked face that went with it.

'Am I hallucinating yet again, or is it the lovely Countess of Repton?'

'It's me, right enough,' Adele smiled through her tears, 'and here to ensure that you take the potions that were prescribed.'

'No more beef tea, though,' William insisted. 'In fact, I believe I can smell venison cooking somewhere, and I finally feel hungry. Did they cook it in honour of your return?'

'No, in honour of mine,' King Richard told him as he moved from the rear of the upper chamber to the bedside. William's eyes opened wider as he struggled to sit up, but Richard raised a hand to restrain him. 'No need for any ceremony, William. I am here solely in order to thank you for your past services, and to reconfirm you as Chief Justice.'

'And to eat my venison,' William joked.

Richard laughed. 'In truth I may not get to do so, since there are so many in the hall below who have come here to wish you a swift recovery. I think I hear even more arriving, so I will go down and keep them in order, leaving you to enjoy your family reunion. Your two sons are hiding behind their mother, and will no doubt wish to add their good wishes.'

Hugh and Robert stepped out of the shadows, and William smiled at Adele. 'I knew that there was a good reason why we didn't have them drowned at birth. They saved my life.'

'Not me,' Hugh admitted. 'That was Robert's doing.'

'And not even me,' Robert added. 'It was those wild outlaws from the woods who you befriended.'

'They deserve a pardon, even assuming that they committed any crimes in the first place,' William nodded.

'King Richard intends to see to that before calling his first council meeting, to which I am invited, although he would not say why,' said Hugh.

'He has advised me,' Adele said, 'and I had rather hoped that he would disclose the reason before he so abruptly took his departure.'

'I did that for a reason,' Richard announced as he reappeared in the doorway, 'and that was to ensure that the latest arrivals were the ones I was awaiting. Your mistress is among them, Adele, and she is asking for you.'

Adele scurried downstairs, leaving Richard to look meaningfully at Hugh.

'You are no doubt expecting to inherit the Earldom of Repton one day, but I have to advise you that I have decided that the title should be inherited by your brother, without whose friends we would not have retaken Nottingham Castle. They will be rewarded in due course, but Robert will have to await his turn. By the look of the colour that has returned to your father's face, this may be some years in the future.'

'Adele would not allow me to die without her permission,' William joked feebly from his bed, 'but is Hugh to go unrewarded for his constant service at your side?'

'Did I say he was?' Richard asked. 'He does not yet know it, but the father-in-law he never met died two weeks ago. He left only one daughter, to whom the estate would ordinarily pass anyway, but in order to leave no doubt in the matter, I hereby appoint him Earl of Flint.'

'You do me great honour, sire,' Hugh murmured.

Richard shook his head. 'I reward men only when they have earned it, Hugh, and if ever a man earned it, it is you. I have also reserved a seat for you on the Council of State that will see to the restoration of the nation after my misguided brother's attempts to rule it. We meet in three days' time, and now you may wish to go downstairs into the hall and reveal those happy tidings to the Countess of Flint.'

It took a moment for Hugh to grasp the import of that last comment, then his eyes widened with delight. He gave a yell of joy as he thundered down the wooden stairs and into the arms of Edwina, who had anticipated his actions and handed baby Geoffrey to Beth.

'Happy families,' Queen Dowager Eleanor observed with a wry smile. 'There was a time that I believed I had raised one.'

The following day, a small group of horsemen trotted their mounts casually up the North Road that was overhung by the early summer foliage of the Shire Wood. King Richard sat in its centre, and to one side rode the newly created Earl of Flint, with Hubert Walter, the newly appointed Justiciar of England, on his other side, bearing a scroll.

'Robert of Swinecote, come out from wherever you're skulking!' Hugh called. 'You may once have been known as "Robin", but you are to be restored to your lands and proper title, along with all your comrades, including the tall one whose head threatens to pierce the sky.'

When that produced no response, he tried again.

'We know that you've been following us since Edwinstowe, because I've spotted some of your men trailing us as they flitted between the trees. The king does not have all day, so cease your games and reveal yourselves!'

The surrounding foliage parted in twenty different places as men dressed in brown and green homespun stepped out into the roadway. Richard raised his hand for his party to rein in their mounts. He was soon surrounded by forty or fifty men as he gave the order for Walter to unroll the parchment he'd been carrying.

'A pardon to all men of late deprived of their lands and titles by the false hand of the pretended King John and his wicked henchmen,' he announced. 'You are hereby declared freemen once again, and may return to your former lands and estates without any fear of let or hindrance. This by my hand, this twelfth day of April in the year of our Lord, 1194. Richard Plantagenet, by the grace of God King of England.'

A rousing cheer went up from the men grouped around them, and Robin stepped forward.

'Our grateful thanks to your most gracious Majesty. Our lives are yours to command whenever you shall require our assistance.'

'Thank you, Robert of Swinecote, as you have once again become. You were once known as "Robin", in which guise you did much to defend my people when it was most required, and I shall not hesitate to call upon you again should the occasion be appropriate. But for now resume your old lives, and put behind you those lives you were forced to live.'

'We shall do so with gratitude, Your Highness,' Robin replied with a slight bow.

Then Richard recalled something. 'I had occasion to describe your exploits to one of my court heralds who fancies himself as a teller of ballads, so perhaps you may find that you pass into folklore under the name you once adopted.'

A NOTE TO THE READER

Dear Reader,

Thank you for taking the time to read this fifth novel in a series of seven that between them cover the twelfth century, a period during which England was transformed beyond recognition. I hope that it lived up to your expectations. Once again the basic plot line was written for me by the events that really happened during one of the most unsettled periods of that tumultuous age.

Richard 'the Lionheart' remains one of the most easily remembered of those monarchs we learned about at school, mainly because of the romantic image of him created by historians who were searching for a hero in an era of English history that was so disrupted and brutal. The reality was that he was a disaster for England.

For the entire ten years of his reign, he was only on English soil for six months. This was not necessarily unusual for the Plantagenet dynasty, since their empire was as much based across the Channel in what we now call France as it was in England — an appendage to the original Norman property portfolio acquired by William the Conqueror. But Richard added to his sins by opening his reign with a dedicated burst of revenue raising by way of taxes and other extortions from subjects who had no interest in what might be happening out in Outremer, as the Holy Land was called in those days. In the process he sold off the most prestigious and powerful offices in the realm, left his ageing mother to control his jealous and untrustworthy young brother John while he played the Christian war hero in an attempt to win back Jerusalem for the

Roman Church, then wondered why it all came apart at the seams.

Likewise his arrogance during the Crusade earned him the burning enmity of those other monarchs of Europe that he had not already alienated, such as Philip of France, whose half-sister Alys was jilted by Richard as an intended bride, to be replaced by Berengaria of Navarre, who earned herself the distinction of being the only Queen of England never to visit it. Little wonder, when Richard returned overland from what in military terms was a failed Crusade, that those powerful leaders he had badly insulted took the opportunity to imprison him and send England the bill. For the second time in his reign, the nation was all but bankrupted in order to pander to his needs.

At the same time, his younger brother John was rated by the same historians as deserving a place at the other end of the public relations spectrum, and we all learned about 'Bad King John'. He was certainly a sadistic megalomaniac — as the next novel in the series, *The Road to Runnymede*, reveals — but it was in his genes. His father Henry II had been merciless to his enemies, and had a vile and unpredictable temper that both brothers inherited, but only John is recorded in popular history texts as displaying the same fault. In fact, a little research reveals several occasions upon which Richard was — in the course of being a 'valiant', 'courageous' and 'fearless' knight — guilty of what today would be classed as 'war crimes' and 'crimes against humanity', but we never got to hear about those.

So what was John supposed to do, when he was urged by Richard's supporters to pull his head in and watch England slide into anarchy and chaos? He was a hopeless administrator, as subsequent events were to prove, and he was feckless, extravagant and treacherous, but was he *really* so bad, when compared with his big brother? I didn't spare his blushes in this novel, but neither did I overplay his role in Richard's misfortunes, most of which were self-inflicted. I couldn't, however, help feeling sorry for their mother.

Into this dynastically dysfunctional saga I inserted a few fictional characters of my own, while also reviving another of history's myths from this era — Robin Hood. If he existed at all, then it most certainly wasn't during the reign of Richard I, although it was the case that the vicious and inhumane 'forest laws' had driven many simple folk off their lands and forced them to hunt the 'royal deer' in order to stave off starvation. As for the so-called 'Sheriff of Nottingham' who features in the folk tales we grew up with, he didn't exist until the mid-fifteenth century, when Nottingham got its first civic charter. Before that date, the villain of the piece would have been the 'High Sheriff of Nottinghamshire, Derbyshire and the Royal Forests' depicted in this novel, who really *was* a man called William de Wendenal. Whether or not he was the unlovable person I described, it is perhaps significant that he disappeared completely from the public records at around the time of Richard's return to England, which suited my storyline very conveniently.

I hope that you are sufficiently encouraged to acquire the next novel in the series, but whether you are or not, I'd love to get feedback from you on this one — or perhaps even a review of it on **Amazon** or **Goodreads**. Or, if you prefer, send your thoughts to me on my author website, **davidfieldauthor.com**.

David

Sapere Books is an exciting new publisher of brilliant fiction and popular history.

To find out more about our latest releases and our monthly bargain books visit our website: **saperebooks.com**